NANTUCKET

HARRISON YOUNG
NANTUCKET

VENTURA

Nantucket by Harrison Young

First published by Ventura Press 2015
PO Box 780 Edgecliff
NSW 2027
AUSTRALIA

www.venturapress.com.au

National Library of Australia Cataloguing-in-Publication entry
Author: Young, Harrison.
Title: Nantucket: where the rich and beautiful come to play/Harrison Young

ISBN: 978-1-925183-31-3 (print edition)
ISBN: 978-1-925183-34-4 (Epub edition)

Cover images: Getty images, iStock
Cover design: Deborah Parry Graphics
Editorial: Amanda Hemmings
Production: Jasmine Standfield
Printed in Australia by McPherson's Printing Group

About the Author

Harrison Young has been writing fiction in airports and on weekends since 1981. Graduating from Harvard University in 1966, Young has been a journalist for *The Washington Post*, a captain in the U.S. Army Special Forces, a government advisor and an investment banker. He has done business in twenty countries and has advised a dozen governments on financial system issues. Young helped establish banks in Bahrain and Beijing and as a senior official at the FDIC in Washington he managed the resolution of 266 failing banks. A dual citizen, Young retired as chairman of Morgan Stanley Australia in 2007 and became a director of Commonwealth Bank of Australia.

1

If the weekend was music, it was a dazzling improvisation: invisible musicians, a theme stated and explored, the violins of reason chasing the cello of desire, sound swelling to fill the house. Andrew wasn't listening when he landed in Nantucket, though. That came later. Understanding came later.

Andrew was quite pleased with himself, in fact, as he got off the plane, accompanied by his two billionaires and their seriously beautiful wives. One of the men owned something the other one wanted – provided the terms were "reasonable" – and had indicated his willingness to talk. Andrew had persuaded them to be his guests for the weekend – his and Cathy's, that is. This was how he made his living.

Andrew had brought the usual financial projections and a handful of power point slides, but he doubted he'd need them. Joe and Shiva could do earnings-per-share dilution calculations in their heads – as could Andrew, of course – but more to the point, the deal in prospect didn't hinge on numbers but on trust. Although Joe's company was the "natural owner" of the intellectual property one of Shiva's companies had developed, and consequently could offer a "competitive" price for it, Shiva would receive more value if the deal was "tax efficient," and the structure most likely to achieve that involved their being partners for a few years. In Andrew's experience, very rich people were reluctant to trust anyone, let alone accept them as partners. Hence the house party.

A house party is a form of theatre: a gathering of friends and strangers resolved to entertain each other, a little version of the world. What happened on this occasion was comic – a sequence of improbable events with a happy ending. But the players themselves didn't know that. When they put on their costumes, everything was at risk.

Comedy is a form of wisdom. It permits outrageousness. We understand ourselves by mocking the blindness of others. We come to terms with life's arbitrary cruelty by laughing at the neatness of the plot. Wisdom can be painful but it doesn't have to be – which is nice to know.

Some house parties are primarily a means of showing off. See my gorgeous sailboat. Guess how much my decorator cost. Investment bankers make a lot of money, but foot soldiers like Andrew cannot win that competition. More importantly, if they're smart, they never forget the famous question, "Where are your customers' yachts, Mr Morgan?" and are modest about whatever wealth they possess.

The world Andrew and Cathy created each summer weekend in Nantucket was designed to make everyone an equal. The corporate chieftains and status-conscious wives they invited were treated like family – expected to help set the table and wash dishes. Some were a bit shocked by this, even at first insulted – they were used to staff and servants – but mostly and in time they found it amusing, even relaxing. They were made to go on walks that wore them out, helped them unwind, and with luck made them friends.

The objective this weekend was more challenging than usual: causing a driven American engineer and an elegant Indian prince to bond. "You're kidding," Cathy had responded when Andrew introduced the idea. "How are you planning to manage that?"

"Same as always," he'd told her. "Make it up as we go along." And so he did.

"We don't need to fall in love," Joe had told Andrew, "but I've got to check him out. I won't say I can read Indians, but I want to at least be sure no alarms go off." And later, after the weekend had been arranged: "You know, Andrew, the thing about Indians is that some of them are saints and some are bandits – I'm talking about the top businessmen, now – and I find it very difficult to tell them apart. They all went to Oxford. They all have wonderful manners and excellent taste. They all have personal charities they support. Some of them fast one day a week, if you can believe it. But you've been to Mumbai, you've seen the poverty, you've read how widows get burned alive, or at least used to. Your brain is telling you the guy you're doing business with is probably in line for the Nobel Peace Prize, but your gut is telling you he'd sell you his wife if that would grease the deal."

"Have you met Rosemary?" Andrew had asked him over the phone. If Rosemary was for sale, she'd be expensive.

"That's Mrs Shiva? No, I've barely shaken hands with *him*, as you know. What's she like? Not Indian, I assume."

"Venus as head prefect." The notion of buying Shiva's wife had lighted a fire in Andrew's brain he was finding hard to put out. He didn't want to put it out, actually.

"English bondage school, eh?" said Joe.

"Yes, and her father's an earl," said Andrew, pretending not to hear the joke. "But that doesn't do her justice. *Lady* Rosemary is the sort of woman wars were fought over, back when that sort of thing happened. Pale skin. White-blonde hair. Long neck. Perfect figure..."

"She turns you on, eh?"

Andrew didn't answer. Perhaps Shiva would give him Rosemary as a "deal toy" – one of those souvenirs that were passed out at closing dinners for major transactions. Andrew had four Montblanc pens, three scale models of Boeing airplanes, and five unopened bottles of Dom Pérignon in his office. A woman would be much more useful. Stop it, he told himself. He was getting over-excited.

Then again, excitement was crucial to getting deals done. You became more creative. You needed less sleep. "Holy madness," Andrew sometimes called it. Not that there was anything holy about the merger business.

"Personally," Joe was saying, "I've never seen the point of English girls. All that Wellies and Barbour crap, standing out in the rain, growling at the dogs and getting excited about a mug of hot cider."

"I take it you've been to a shooting party."

"Once. I've been to everything once. You get high enough on the *Forbes* 'Rich List' and everyone but the Pope wants to entertain you." Joe had paused. "No offence, Andrew. This weekend with you and Cathy has a purpose. And I'm kind of curious to see where Moby Dick came from. Or to be accurate, where Ahab came from and Ishmael found a ship. The whale came from the Great Southern Ocean.

"Anyway, it was grouse we were supposed to be shooting, only I couldn't hit any. The whole weekend seemed to be a continuous in-joke. There was a girl I was expected to go after. This was before Cynthia, you understand."

"But after Martha," said Andrew.

"And Tina," said Joe.

Joe had an "efficient" approach to marriage, as he put it. Andrew had summarised the matter for Cathy. "He knows what he wants, or he says he does. He insists on a pre-nup. If the woman delivers, great. If it doesn't work out, she walks away with $100 million."

"Hard to resist," Cathy had said.

Maybe he could sell Cathy to Joe. If Joe was interested in bondage, Cathy would be ideal. Their marriage was a form of bondage. But so are many people's marriages. Or so Andrew told himself.

"After dinner I went upstairs and crashed," Joe continued, "which wasn't hard after standing around in the cold all day. When I came down to breakfast, the hostess was mad at me. I was supposed to have realised the girl had the best guest room for a reason."

Andrew had been to that sort of English weekend once himself. The memory of it was a pillar of his Anglophilia – and a well-spring of guilt. He'd been at the investment banking firm where he'd made his career for a little more than a year. He was twenty-two. The firm had sent him to the London office to crunch numbers on a deal. It was supposed to be for a week but it turned into a month. "It's a good sign," he'd told Cathy, who was stuck in Brooklyn with their six-month-old daughter. The guys in the London office wanted to give him a good time, so they arranged to have the client entertain him. Or maybe he was being hazed. He was pretty green. "Be amusing," he was told. "Your host is important."

Long train ride to the north. No idea where he was. A cold wind that chilled him as he waited to be picked up. His hostess arrived fifteen minutes late, apologised profusely, drove way too fast for the narrow roads, apologised further that the roster · of guests kept changing, with the result that she now needed to ask him, would he mind sharing a bathroom with another guest? Of course he wouldn't. "You'll have your own bedroom, of course," his hostess had said.

The bathroom was between, and only accessible from, the two bedrooms. There were no locks. He was warming up by taking a strongly recommended pre-dinner bath in the enormous tub when his neighbour came in. "I'm told there's a hot water shortage," she'd said, hanging her dressing gown on a hook on the door and climbing in so she faced him. "I hope you don't mind my joining you."

"Delighted," Andrew had said, trying to be casual about it.

"Oh, aren't you nice," she said, as if his erection was a form of good manners. "I'm Venetia, by the way." She held out her hand.

"I'm Andrew," he said.

"And you're an American, I take it. Have you been to one of these things before? Here, let me wash your back."

"Never," he said, turning around.

"Well, the men compete to see who can shoot the most pheasants, and the ladies compete to see who can bag the most men."

"In a weekend?"

"A proper test match lasts five days, but yes."

"You are making this up, I assume."

"Didn't Francis tell you?"

"No. And neither did Frances." One of the many

disconcerting features of the weekend was that his host and hostess had the same name, though with different spellings. The British loved double entendre, he had found.

"Well, they both keep game books," said Venetia. "But here's the deal. You're a banker, right? Presumably you know about deals. I'm at Sotheby's. I know about furniture. Now you do me." She turned around without giving him a chance to answer, which was helpful. It still made him self-conscious to call himself a banker and it definitely made him self-conscious to be rubbing her shoulders with soapy hands. She was probably a few years older than he was. "There is no central heating," she continued. "Frances believes central heating is non-U. You know about U and non-U, I assume. No? It's such fun when the American knows nothing. Nancy Mitford's coinage. 'U' for upper class. Anyway, the water in your wash basin will probably freeze overnight. You don't have to fuck *any*one, but you are well advised to share a bed with *some*one."

"Right," Andrew said.

"To be honest," said Venetia. "Lower back, please. Yes. *Yes.* Now rinse me off. To be honest, I hope you'll share mine. I've never bagged an American." Before he could respond, she was out of the tub and had opened the door into her bedroom. A cloud of cold air rolled in, followed by another English beauty. "This is Anne," said Venetia. "Her bedroom only has a shower. But you've got to get out now. I'm not letting you touch her."

"Oh, unfair," said Anne, taking off her robe.

"Get dressed quickly, Andrew," said Venetia, "or you'll freeze to death. And remember, we have an understanding."

That weekend was where Andrew had gotten the idea of using house parties as a business development tool, though it was a dozen years before he had the money to buy the right sort of house. Generally speaking, it had been a good strategy. *This* weekend was likely to be hard work, though. The elan necessary to amuse billionaires was hard to generate if your wife wasn't enthusiastic, and recently Cathy hadn't been much fun – on edge most of the time. He hadn't had much time to talk to her about her moods. But if he had to be charming for both of them, well, he had to.

He'd tuned back in on Joe. "'Look, I told the hostess,'" Joe was saying, "'I'm an American. I miss a lot. But if it would help, I'll stay in this morning.' It was pelting rain, you understand. 'I'll claim I have a cold. She can stay back to look after me. Satisfaction guaranteed. Her name's Lavinia, right?'

"Hostess very offended. Lavinia had left already. Her horse was alleged to be sick."

Andrew had laughed. "It must be hard having fifteen billion dollars." And to himself: perhaps that's a requirement for a proper English house partyparty – there should be a naive American for one of the girls to lay.

"Oh, it's all right," Joe had said. "But if there's someone I'm supposed to sleep with, just tell me. Except when it involves money, I'm pretty accommodating."

"Cynthia would be a good choice," Andrew had said without thinking about it.

"That's why I married her. I decided I wanted to sleep with her. Good-looking girl, don't you think? Bit of glamour, her being a TV star. A news anchor's a star, right, even if her show is in the morning?"

"Most of America knows her name," said Andrew, "and probably a quarter of them wake up by listening to her." It struck him that Joe regarded his wives as a series of venture capital investments.

"Third time lucky, I hope," said Joe. "And come to think of it, Cyn spent a year as an exchange student in England. Her father wanted to make her posh, I guess. She knows how to play field hockey. She can kick me under the table if I say something wrong.

"You know, the funny thing is," Joe continued, "I began to think that Lavinia chick was fairly attractive once she'd left. I liked the way she didn't put up with any crap. Just got in her car and drove home. That was the trouble with Tina, I realised. She was always trying too hard to please me, asking me what I wanted. I have enough decisions to make at work without having to be in charge of where we go for dinner."

Joe did the dumb country boy routine pretty well, in Andrew's opinion. It helped that he was six foot four and never looked comfortable in a suit. It helped that he was completely unembarrassed about sex.

"You'll think he's a jock until you discover how smart he is," Andrew had told Cathy. "Big hands. Big shoulders. Powerful body. Has to have his suits made. Women probably find him attractive, and not just for the money. But if you *can't* see him – like when talking on the phone – you start thinking he's a nerd. Gobbles up information like a lumberjack eating breakfast. He knows everything there is to know about the patents Shiva controls. Refers to them by number. He can take you through the tax strategy like he's negotiating rapids in a kayak.

"The only thing he hasn't worked out yet is Shiva himself, and he's doing the research. Probably knows his blood type by now. Is Shiva reliable? The answer is mostly, by the way. Is Shiva a criminal? No one seems to think so. What are his hobbies? Vintage cars, supposedly. Showing off his education is what I'd say. Does he have any weaknesses? Whispers about imaginative sex, but I suspect that's just other people fantasising."

"So why do they have to spend the weekend with us?" Cathy had asked.

"Well, for starters, Shiva needs to check out Joe, though he'd never say that."

"Shiva hasn't done the research?"

"Probably done some – or had it done for him. We have to pretend this weekend is purely social, by the way. No 'commerce' involved."

"Which is bullshit," said Cathy. It was a pretence that governed most of their house parties, which for some reason had always offended Cathy.

"We let Joe and Shiva decide when to admit that," said Andrew. There seemed to be an argument they needed to have soon.

"To be honest, it is very difficult to figure out what Shiva knows. Or thinks. He turns the charm on and off as it suits him. Same for temper tantrums."

"He'd better not try that with me."

"The trick," Andrew lectured – he'd told her all this before – "the trick is not to take it personally. You have to view him as a machine that occasionally does strange things, and try to figure out how the mechanism works."

"Is that how you see me?" said Cathy.

"Shiva has a massive sense of entitlement," Andrew continued, ignoring her question. "He had an employee who figured out a way to save him fifty million dollars. Joe unearthed this story. The man asked for a modest raise. Shiva was genuinely shocked. He'd given the man the job that allowed him to score goals. Shiva therefore owned the goals. But many successful entrepreneurs are like that. With Shiva, there's other stuff going on. It may have to do with his ancestry, which he tells me he can trace back a couple of thousand years.

"On the plus side, he seems to be genuinely pleased to be spending the weekend with us. I assume he had to twist Rosemary's arm. 'A magical island,' he calls Nantucket, 'somewhere out in the vast Atlantic.' He wants to know if there will be sprites and monsters, wants me to show him 'the local Caliban,' as he puts it. Can you think of any candidates?"

"Fresh out of monsters," said Cathy. "But did you tell Shiva Nantucket is only thirty miles from Cape Cod? Or that *The Tempest*, to which I take it he's referring, was inspired by the discovery of *Bermuda*?"

"Never be smarter than the client," said Andrew, repeating a maxim he sometimes had trouble obeying. "It was Rosemary who told him where Shakespeare got the idea – when we had dinner in London."

"So she likes to parade her erudition too."

"*Please* don't be touchy, sweetheart." For just a moment neither of them spoke. Cathy had dropped out of college to marry Andrew, and produced Eleanor almost immediately. For some stupid reason she had an inferiority complex about her lack of a diploma, which no amount of reading could overcome. Andrew himself had been Phi Beta Kappa at Harvard, which he endeavoured never to mention. "But yes," he continued. "Rosemary got first-class honours at Cambridge, I fear. She wants to go to the whaling museum, by the way."

"Part of the package," said Cathy.

"I should warn you that Shiva continues to call me 'Prospero.'"

"Sounds like if he believes something, that makes it true," said Cathy.

"Bit of that," Andrew had said. "But remember, you don't have to like him, just be nice to him. And tell me what you think when you've met him."

"I'll do my best," Cathy had said.

For obvious reasons, the weekend needed to be perfect. But Andrew and Cathy were good at this sort of thing.

Their house was a classic "shore colonial" – unpainted pine shingles that had turned grey, with white trim that had to be refreshed every other year. It had five bedrooms, spacious porches where you could sit and play scrabble when it rained, easy access to the ocean when it was sunny. In the time before air-conditioning, when Broadway theatres closed for the summer months, it had been part of a noted actors' colony. Its relatively isolated location, on the ridge at the eastern edge of the island, threw its occupants together and required them to perform.

Andrew saw himself as an impresario – a profession requiring both vision and nerve. He booked airplane tickets twelve months in advance, and spent each fall and winter deciding who it would pay to entertain. If Cathy grew weary, which to be fair hadn't been often, he'd remind her that "your skill as a hostess and my brass balls are what put our daughters through college." Nine months earlier, Joe and Shiva had never heard of Andrew. Didn't know each other either. He'd talked them into separate meetings with him on the strength of an idea. By the end of the year he hoped to send each of them a bill for ten million dollars.

A big fee would be quite helpful, to be honest. He hadn't brought one in for a couple of years. The men who ran his firm were reasonable, but Wall Street is Wall Street. The unspoken question, "Is Andrew losing his edge?" would get asked soon enough.

Andrew hadn't discussed compensation with either house guest yet. The time to do that was *after* the weekend, when the fact of his having brought them together would be irrefutable. Joe would agree immediately. Shiva would try to negotiate, but would fold when Andrew pointed out that Joe had already agreed. Then when they got to documenting the transaction, Joe (or more accurately, his lawyers) would be difficult, and Shiva would have to ask him to lighten up. That's how he read them, anyway. Andrew prided himself on reading people.

Going down the steps from the plane, Andrew scanned the crowd of wives waiting behind the waist-high chain link fence at the edge of the airfield. No Cathy. Bad form, her being late. That hadn't happened before. But no doubt there would be an explanation. Andrew told himself not to be grumpy. All it would do was show he was anxious. Mustn't be anxious.

One of Cathy's party tricks was to meet the plane from New York with a thermos of gin and tonic, which she served to arriving guests in plastic cups. "House rules," she'd tell anyone who was reluctant. "You're on holiday. And make the men take off their neckties." It would spoil the effect, though, if she was late.

A moment later, Andrew spotted Sally, the au pair. She was holding the thermos and a stack of cups. She appeared to be wearing one of Cathy's loose-fitting, brightly coloured summer dresses. No doubt there would be an explanation for that as well. In any event, she seemed to have collected Shiva and Rosemary, who'd been seated further forward in the plane and would have been easy to identify. Andrew suggested Joe and Cynthia join them and went to organise the luggage.

The "au pair" was an innovation. Andrew was, to be

honest, slightly disconcerted by her. Something about the way she moved, the way she did things – rearranged the refrigerator, ate a raw carrot while she fried mushrooms, perched on the porch railing reading a magazine – every gesture told you she was in charge. She struck him as a free spirit. There weren't a lot of free spirits in his world. But with Cathy being for some reason delayed at home, it was certainly convenient to have employed her. In contrast to the high-school girls they'd had when their daughters were young, Sally was a safe driver and a capable cook. She was teaching Cathy to draw. They went running together. And she was nice to look at. Joe and Shiva would both like that.

The reason they'd hired Sally was basically that Cathy was afraid of being lonely. Cathy had turned thirty-nine that April. Andrew was forty-two. Their daughters had grown up, or were trying to. Florence had finished her first year of college and had met a boy who looked like a "keeper" – as she and her friends called potential husbands – so she'd found a summer job in San Francisco that allowed her to be near him, with the result that she wouldn't be in Nantucket.

"And Eleanor?" Andrew had asked.

"We've been through all that," Cathy had said.

"She's decided to hate us."

"She needs to become her own person."

"It's fine if she hates us, you know, so long as she gets over it. Which she will – probably by September but certainly within a year. What was it she said at that very dramatic family lunch we had on your birthday? I'm a blood-sucking investment banker and you're a what?"

"A trivial woman who never finished college," Cathy said evenly.

"Sorry."

"But even if she finishes hating us early," said Cathy, "she's in Munich…"

"In a job I got her…"

"Which she hates you for – with me as collateral damage." At this point Cathy had wiped away a genuine tear. "Oh, sweetie, I am just trying to say that I will not do well in that big empty house."

"Well, we have to be in Nantucket," Andrew had said, less softly than he meant to.

"Yes, I know. There are people coming to stay. You've invited them already. We entertain well. You always do bring interesting people, and only a few of them have made passes at me…"

"Which ones?"

"It doesn't matter."

"It does to me."

"They were easy enough to fend off."

"Men or women?"

"*Men*, sweetie. What are you thinking?" And then, in a teasing voice: "There was one woman, actually. She was going through a bad patch in her marriage. I found her whimpering in the living room when I came downstairs for a glass of milk at three in the morning. She needed to be kissed, she said."

"And you accommodated her?"

"Mostly it was a hug. I'm a good hostess. I'm making this all up, you realise. I know it turns you on. But, Andrew, that's not the point. The point is what the fuck will I do from Monday morning or even Sunday evening when I put you and our invariably interesting house guests on the plane back to New York, until seven-whatever on Friday evening, when I show up with the gin and tonic?"

"If there's too much work, hire a maid," he'd responded. "Or hire an au pair." Not actually a sensible suggestion. One of Andrew's bad habits was shooting from the hip, but it was a bad habit he shared with most members of his profession.

"Au pairs are for children, Andrew, which as you may recall I am going to be without."

"You always said the au pairs we hired were children themselves."

"That's not what I want, Andrew."

"What *do* you want?"

"Someone to talk to. A local to help clean the house isn't enough. More of a companion than a servant."

"Do it," Andrew had said. "Pay over the odds if you need to. It's got to be an attractive gig. Cooking and light housekeeping. Room with your own bath. But she has to be willing to take her days off in the middle of the week and work when our guests are here."

"So I can sit on the porch and be glamorous?" said Cathy, recovering slightly. It was a joke between them. Cathy had been a pretty girl, and she'd kept her figure, but there was always a stain on her tee shirt or a bath towel on the floor to remind them both she hadn't stepped off the pages of *Vogue*. Or perhaps it was some sort of protest. "Age?"

"What?"

"This woman who's going to keep me company, how old do you want her to be?"

"Thirty-five. A grown-up but younger than us."

"I suppose you'd want her to be attractive."

Andrew hadn't answered that. "Talk to the agencies that supply nannies," he'd said.

"Blonde, dark hair or red-head?" Cathy had continued.

"Dark and mysterious," he replied. Cathy liked it, sometimes, when he shot from the hip.

"Skinny or voluptuous?"

"Oh, both."

"Will you want to sleep with her?"

"Of course, but I won't."

"Fair enough," Cathy had said. "Do you mind if I do?"

Andrew had laughed – and forgotten all about the matter until he arrived on the evening plane the guest-free first weekend of the season, and there the two of them were in sandals and billowing dresses, looking like sisters or girlfriends. "This is Sally," Cathy had said. "We drove up together on Tuesday. The house looks great."

Sally had smiled and handed him a gin and tonic.

This weekend's house guests all seemed to have accepted their gin and tonics and were presumably playing "who do you know"? which very rich people find gratifying as they tend to know celebrities. Joe and Cynthia had gotten to the airport at the very last minute, so this would be their first chance to play. Then again, maybe they didn't need to. Cynthia was a celebrity herself, after all.

Sally was walking away from them and towards Andrew, bringing his drink. She came up quite close to him. It wasn't unpleasant having her in his personal space but it disconcerted him. That word again. He accepted his drink. She began to remove his necktie and unbutton his shirt collar.

"Listen carefully," she said. "I have to talk fast. Cathy has gone to Munich. Your older daughter is having some sort of emotional crisis…"

"Why didn't Cathy call me…?" He started to pull out his

mobile phone but she grabbed his wrist to stop him.

"Just listen. Cathy gave me a note, which you need to read. She said this weekend is very important and that her not being here could screw things up. She said it could cost you twenty million dollars, but I expect she was exaggerating."

"Only slightly," said Andrew.

"She said Eleanor is fine, just demanding attention, but she felt she had to go. She said she'd be a lousy hostess anyway if she stayed. I drove her to catch the last ferry to Boston, which left while you were in the air. A flight from Boston seemed to be the way to get to Germany fastest."

Andrew started to interrupt again but Sally took hold of his arm and cut him off. "Don't argue. Just listen."

He acquiesced. She had strong hands, and no hesitation about touching him, he noticed.

"The point is," Sally continued, "she's right. So far, your guests think I'm Cathy." Sally paused. "It can work. I know the house. Her clothes fit me. I've hidden all the framed photographs of Cathy. But you need to decide how you want to play this in the next fifteen seconds. Here's the note."

Andrew unfolded the paper and recognised his wife's handwriting. "Sally will explain," the note said. "She knows everything. Don't call. Don't even think about me. I'll call when I can. Cathy."

Looking over Sally's shoulder, he could see Joe and Shiva coming towards them, presumably to help with the luggage, which was sitting on a cart that had just arrived outside the tiny terminal.

"So?" said Sally.

"I'm in your hands," said Andrew.

"Sorry, Cathy," said Joe, coming up to them. "We forgot

our manners."

"Rosemary says we mustn't forget the cheese," said Shiva. He explored the pile of suitcases and extracted a plain cardboard box tied up with dark red ribbons.

"Ooo, I know that wrapping," said Sally.

"I'll hold it for you until we get to the house," said Rosemary, who had now joined the group, leaving Cynthia on her own some yards away.

For an unguarded moment, the American girl looked vaguely troubled. Yes, that was the word for it. Then she was composed and patient again – the "talent" waiting for the camera crew to do their jobs. She was startlingly slender, as television required, with hair that stayed in place despite the wind, a tailored beige dress made of a fabric that didn't wrinkle, and, as a concession to Nantucket, open-toed shoes. It occurred to Andrew that in whatever game of one-upmanship was going on, Cynthia must have lost the first set. She didn't look like she planned to lose the match, though. Rosemary had a title, but Cynthia had an Emmy. Have to think about it later.

"No, no, I've got them," Andrew said to Shiva, hanging onto the Indian couple's soft leather bags, which must have cost tens of thousands of pounds. "I never bring a suitcase myself."

"What a luxury," said Shiva.

"You should try it," said Joe. "I buy three of everything – for Greenwich, Palo Alto and Shanghai."

"What do you travel in?" said Shiva. He himself was wearing grey trousers and a pink silk shirt that would have looked absurd on an American.

"Blue jeans," said Joe, looking down at himself, "plus running shoes, a tee shirt, and a very experienced navy blue jacket."

"You know," said Shiva, "I have never in my life worn blue jeans."

All three men laughed.

"Look at what Rosemary's brought," said Sally to Cynthia when they all got to the car. "Just seeing those red ribbons makes my mouth water." They were the signature of a shop called "The Madison Avenue Cheesemonger." Andrew had walked past it but never gone in.

Cynthia made an equivocal noise.

"Right," said Sally. "I haven't had a drink so I'll drive. Joe, you're the biggest, so you ride shotgun. You said you'd brought a map, so we'll pretend you're the navigator."

"He'll like that," said Cynthia, "though I promise you, the map fetish gets boring fast."

"Will he like it if you sit on Shiva?" said Sally. "Rosemary and the cheese need their own seat. Andrew has to perch between you, and anyway, he's too bony to sit on."

"Did our hostess just say I'm fat?" said Shiva.

"Supple," said Rosemary, as Cynthia climbed onto Shiva with what looked like mixed emotions.

"All aboard," said Sally.

Andrew sat in the uncomfortable middle seat, full of hope, a little boy inexplicably allowed to play with the big kids. He probably shouldn't have been an investment banker, he told himself. He wasn't an athlete – or any kind of team player, really – in a profession that revered sports and spoke in sports metaphors. He had entered the arena without the endowment of ruthlessness so many of his colleagues had grown up with. He didn't relish mayhem. An only child, he didn't have close friends. Cathy was...Cathy. He had taught himself to be a good host, but through preparation rather than exuberance: plenty of sunscreen, spare clothes, knowing it was someone's birthday. He had devised a career that allowed him to work alone – sitting quietly in his office conceiving an astounding merger as his colleagues shouted joyful obscenities in the hall, riding an elevator to the lair of a terrifying chief executive armed with a single sheet of paper, being delivered to the crucial meeting in a corporate jet. He was a lonely man in a profession that required optimism.

But he was smart and persistent and brave, and that seemed to have been enough. There was no way of knowing what the next forty-eight hours would bring, he reflected – and he took comfort from that thought. He had been improvising for twenty years.

2

A lot of what worked in Andrew and Cathy's marriage was stuff they didn't talk about. Like whether he and Cathy had sex on any particular night. They had come to an understanding that she initiated. It was another of their "house rules," though the understanding was never discussed, devoid of "legislative history," as a lawyer might put it. Andrew thought maybe Cathy thought it was his way of doing penance for so often being quick on the trigger, sarcastic, inconsiderate – for being the sort of man Wall Street demanded. Or for that month in London, which she'd never really asked about. But he also knew that he found it erotic to cede control. And he liked to tell himself that she found making him wait erotic. So when Sally walked into their bedroom and started to undress as if it was no big deal, she was putting on Cathy's persona even as she took off her clothes.

Sally had shooed everyone upstairs with the statement that dinner would be served in about an hour, and that she assumed they'd all like showers. Andrew was sitting on a chair beside the bow window with a view of the ocean, waiting for their guests to finish. If too many people took showers at once the pressure dropped. He'd wrapped a towel around his waist on the assumption that Sally might come in.

"You'd better get used to this if we're going to pretend we're married," said Sally.

"Used to what?" said Andrew. He forced himself to look at her.

"Intimacy without sex," she said, taking off Cathy's dress. "Your wife has some very nice things, by the way."

"What's the boundary?"

"Get on the bed. On your front. I'll massage your back a bit. You're so tense I can feel it from here."

Andrew did as he was told, discarding the towel as he got on the bed. Sally started to work on his shoulders. "You didn't answer my question," said Andrew into the pillow.

"Lie still. What question?"

"What's the boundary between intimacy and sex?

"Orgasm," she said. "Yours, that is."

There was a brief pause in the conversation, as Sally worked her knuckles down Andrew's spine. "Why did you put Cynthia on Shiva's lap?" he said finally.

"To see what tension it created."

"And the answer was?"

"Well, it didn't seem to bother Joe at all. What did you observe? Nice ass, by the way."

"Thanks." That seemed the appropriate response.

"I am to some extent a connoisseur of bottoms," said Sally cheerfully.

"Have you been in the spanking business?" said Andrew, surprising himself.

Sally paused briefly and then laughed. "No comment," she said.

"I'm afraid I didn't learn anything from your experiment with the seating arrangements," he said. "I had a lot on my mind."

"Of course you did," said Sally. Just for a moment Andrew nearly swooned as her sympathy made his whole body relax. "But I need to ask you a few things about this weekend. Like, whose side are we on?"

"Ah," said Andrew, spying safer ground. "Both sides. We are friends of the deal. I get a fee from both of them if it happens. My firm does, that is."

"Is that the usual arrangement?"

"No. You normally work for one side or the other. But even then, your job can be helping your client agree to pay enough."

"You only get paid if the deal happens?"

"Yes. That's why it's called a 'success fee.'"

"So you're giving advice but you aren't at all disinterested?"

"Isn't that how life works? No one's disinterested."

"Why so cynical?"

"Twenty years as an investment banker. You see the underside of people."

"So how come you aren't unfaithful?"

"How do you know I'm not?"

"You're afraid of me, that's one way. You're afraid of this situation."

I'm not afraid, he wanted to say but didn't. Just anxious. There was a lot at stake. But then, if he was to be honest, he'd been anxious his whole life.

"And Cathy told me what you're like," Sally continued.

"Annoying but virtuous?"

"Oh, she told me a lot more than that."

"About what?"

"Your sex life, of course. What do you think women talk about?"

Never asked myself that question, Andrew said to himself.

"Cathy and I had a few glasses of wine after we got the house ready. I'd say she told me everything."

"Oh, Jesus."

"I think she found it quite cathartic, analysing you in a clinical way. Of course, she couldn't have known this was going to happen."

"No," said Andrew, "though people often know more than they admit."

"But in the event," she said, "it's useful background. For me, that is." She said nothing for a while as she worked on the small of his back. His glutes were beginning to feel neglected. He wouldn't mind it if she worked on them a bit – but he couldn't think of an appropriate way to suggest it. "So when we get in bed tonight," Sally said, "and I *don't* roll over and touch you, I will *know* that I'm punching all your buttons."

"Oh my," said Andrew. "I'm paying you to torment me, am I?"

"And amuse your guests and keep your secrets."

Somewhere in the house, the sound of showers running stopped. Sally stopped massaging him. "Think of it this way," she said. "Suffering instructs." She gave him a single smack on the bottom and stood up. It didn't hurt. "Playful" would be a good description, he decided. Flirtatious?

Sally said she should probably take the first shower and thoughtfully draped his bath towel over him. He briefly considered calling Cathy's mobile – it was, honestly, the first chance he'd had – but he hesitated. Her plane would have taken off, wouldn't it? Not necessarily. He took refuge in the thought that Cathy had said he should concentrate on his guests – and that Sally would disapprove. No stepping out of character, she'd probably say. She'd never said she was an actress but it felt like she was. Or a director maybe. Something in show business.

She was doing a damn good job of being Cathy. Fact was, she did a better job of it than Cathy had recently. Now that he had his two billionaires under his roof he could acknowledge how worried he had been that Cathy was going to torpedo the event.

The thing was, Cathy could be totally charming when she liked the clients she was required to entertain. She'd hand out buckets and gardening trowels and announce a beachcombing contest – all treasures to be displayed at noon, extra points if you make up a good story about them – and he would get a glimpse of the girl he had met when she had a summer job as a nanny on the Jersey shore right after he graduated from college. His parents had had a house on the Jersey shore – well, they'd rented the same house every July.

Spit it out, he told himself: graduated from *Harvard*. Why should it have to be his fault he was proud of his accomplishments?

Sally came out of the shower, reminding Andrew briefly of the lost Venetia. "Nice breeze," she said, standing in front of the open window without a towel. "I love the way the temperature falls as the sun goes down."

"One of the benefits of being on an island," said Andrew, hauling himself up and going into the bathroom to take his shower. "No man is an island" floated through his mind. Donne on death. His head was full of useless quotations the way some little boys knew baseball statistics.

"Don't be long, sweetheart," Sally called after him. As the

door clicked shut his brain kicked up a sudden painful imagining of Cathy and Sally sitting at the kitchen table, exhausted from two cathartic days of scrubbing and cleaning, making a meal of bread and cheese and peaches, a bottle of red between them. *I call him "sweetheart,"* Cathy is saying. *I make sure he buys new shirts when the old ones wear out – he has this belief that frayed shirts are an emblem of WASP high culture, of not needing to prove your social status – so I have to be sure he doesn't look like an emeritus professor, which is not the path to fame and fortune in his profession – that's if you can call it a profession rather than a branch of organised crime, as our daughter seems to feel – sorry, I'm wandering – anyway, I do what I can to make him happy, but I'm not sure it's working any more.*

The movie screen in Andrew's head went blank before he heard Sally's imagined response. The thought arose that perhaps Sally had murdered Cathy with the intention of taking her place. She was cool enough for it. Powerful wrists, which would be good for strangling. The idea seemed a bit clichéd, though. Andrew briefly glimpsed a Cockney policeman telling the suave detective that the heroine had been "done away with" – but that was replaced with the realisation that Cathy only called him "sweetheart" when *she* was unhappy.

Don't be silly. Just think about making dinner work, he instructed himself, as he turned on the shower. What do Joe and Shiva need to discover? Or their stunning wives?

That could be tricky. He remembered Cynthia looking unhappy at the airport. Cathy got that look sometimes, when she didn't know he was watching her – biting her lip, a million miles away. He hoped Cynthia wasn't going to be Banquo's ghost all weekend – just to weave in another of Shakespeare's plays – the guest who wasn't there, the product of a guilty conscience. There was nothing that could have happened yet to make Cynthia unhappy – nothing Andrew was responsible for anyway. Although on the other hand, he supposed he was responsible for Cathy's whole unhappy life.

3

Andrew always did the *placement* for dinners, which could be quite an enjoyable challenge if you had a dozen guests, changed people's seats after the main course, had to let undistinguished guest B, who might have some business for you and was dying to meet guest A, sit near enough to talk to him, had to let guest A, who was the star of the night, sit near enough to guest X, who was either beautiful or amusing, to enjoy himself and accept your invitations in the future, and mustn't ask anyone to sit next to his own wife because that was middle-class. But with only six people at the table there was no problem to solve. The stunning wives went on either side of him, the billionaires on either side of Sally, and since everyone could talk to everyone, you didn't need to move people. One tiny issue was that, with only four guests, one husband and wife had to sit to the right of both the host and the hostess, which raised a question of status. But Andrew thought that should be easy in this case. Joe didn't care about status. The only thing he believed in was money and he treated his fifteen billion dollars as a happy accident. It didn't matter to him whether Shiva was worth ten billion or twenty billion. Or at least he wanted you to think so. And

Shiva's wealth was so enshrouded with holding companies and tax structures and the claims of litigious half-brothers, that even *Forbes* admitted its ranking of the Indian was a guess. So Lady Rosemary would go on his right and Cynthia on his left. Done.

Andrew allowed himself to think about Rosemary for another minute, though, as he dressed slowly and Sally presumably readied dinner. He'd told Joe that Rosemary was Helen of Troy, essentially – not that Joe would have understood the reference. But Helen had been a young woman when she eloped with Paris and "launched a thousand ships," as Marlowe put it. Rosemary was in her late thirties, just a bit younger than Cathy. Andrew had looked it up. She was becoming transcendentally beautiful in the way some fortunate women do in early middle age. He'd seen her once before, by candlelight at that dinner in London. This afternoon he had studied her in waning sunlight, as they'd all been fussing with the luggage and the expensive cheese and who should sit on whom. She stood so straight. Her features were so perfect. But there was irony in her smile. There were tiny smile lines at the corners of her eyes. She'd allowed herself to be sunburnt in her youth, and it was starting to show. Standing next to her husband, pale pink and mahogany, she reminded Andrew of a prize-winning rose surrendering its petals, scattering beauty and sorrow on the table where it has been displayed. Not in Andrew's league, to be clear about it.

The only problem with Andrew's seating plan was that Cynthia didn't come down for dinner. Or not when everyone else did. "She's doing yoga," Joe apologised to the others, who'd stood up in response to the hostess's announcement that dinner was served.

"She says being in that little tiny airplane we came in gave her a crick in the neck," Joe continued. "Cyn comes from Texas and she thinks everything should be big."

Andrew didn't have a fix yet on what his guests would consider vulgar. He prayed silently that Sally wouldn't say anything salacious, but she didn't even smile. Lady Rosemary, on the other hand, laughed out loud. So much for graceful surrender. "Kick her, please, Andrew," said Shiva. Rosemary subsided.

"Anyway," said Joe, "Cyn insists a couple of dozen pretzel postures will be required before she's fit company for you nice people. So I think we should start, and when she comes downstairs we just pretend she isn't late. In my experience that's the best strategy."

"When did you work that strategy out and would you explain it to Shiva?" said Rosemary.

"About the third day of our honeymoon," said Joe, "but I doubt I could teach Shiva anything about handling women." Joe didn't actually wink at his fellow billionaire, but it felt like he had.

"You are too kind," said Shiva, accepting the compliment. "But to me, what makes women delightful is that I can never figure them out."

"What he means," said Rosemary, sitting down at the table, "is that I can beat him at chess." She'd taken the place of honour automatically, Andrew observed.

"I'll bet he lets you win," said Joe.

Rosemary didn't respond to that.

"If it would help," said Sally, "I could give Cynthia a bit of a massage. Andrew can tell you that I do that pretty well."

"I'll bet you do," said Joe, studying Sally with genuine interest. "But it would just encourage her."

"Yoga is best," said Shiva, as if that would settle the matter, and happily it did.

Cynthia descended before they'd finished the crab salad. She was wearing a cream-colour combination of slacks and what Andrew would have called a tee shirt except that it was obviously cashmere. Shiva stood up and pulled out her chair. "Oh, thank you," she murmured. Her gold chain bracelet clinked on the table as she sat down. Sally went to retrieve her plate from the kitchen. Andrew reached for the champagne beside him in the ice bucket.

"Nothing to drink, please, Andrew," said Cynthia. She's going to play innocent to Rosemary's sophisticated, Andrew decided.

"Another affectation, if you ask me," said Joe.

"On the contrary," said Shiva. "Abstinence is holiness." Andrew noticed that Shiva hadn't touched his wine.

"Well, I can take it or leave it," said Joe. "I never drink when I'm doing business. But this weekend's just fun, right Shiva?"

The Indian had already turned to Cynthia. "The right strategy, if I may suggest, is to let them fill your glass but then not touch it. Otherwise people keep offering it to you and you keep having to refuse, which seems impolite."

Andrew guessed that Cynthia was younger than Rosemary. She was more conventionally beautiful, but less alluring. It was hard to know what you really thought of someone you saw all the time on television. Andrew suspected her late arrival had more to do with getting her hair and make-up right than it did with muscle spasms, but perhaps he was being unkind.

"So Andrew," said Rosemary, cutting through, "who do you like in the Senate race this fall?"

"You mean in Connecticut?" A new worry blossomed in Andrew's brain.

"No," she said. "Massachusetts. Nantucket is part of Massachusetts, isn't it? And there's a Senate race, I'm told."

"There is not. But I vote in New York. We vote in New York. That's our primary residence." He wanted to get away from Massachusetts. The Governor of Massachusetts, who would probably challenge for the Senate seat in two years, had been a classmate. He'd half promised, which was the most you ever got out of George, to stop by for a drink on Sunday, which Andrew had assumed would excite his guests. Some people thought the Governor would run for President eventually. The problem was that George knew Cathy. They came from the same classy suburb of Boston.

"Rosemary has been reading the newspapers," said Shiva, as if that were an odd thing to do. "Her grandmother taught her to do that in preparation for any dinner party. You mustn't run out of things to talk about, the old countess taught her. *My* grandmother, on the other hand, had no opinions regarding dinner parties. She refused to go to them. She regarded eating as obscene..."

"Was she anorexic?" said Cynthia, interrupting.

"Probably," said Rosemary.

"She did, however," Shiva continued, "teach me to prepare for any visit by contemplating the spirit of the place. So I have been reading about the pilgrims. Massachusetts was founded by pilgrims, which makes it a holy place."

"Oh, I like that," said Cynthia, looking at Shiva.

"Nantucket was founded by Quakers, actually," said Andrew, forgetting himself. "They didn't get along with the Puritans."

"Joe would have been a good Quaker," said Cynthia quietly, keeping a straight face as Shiva laughed.

"Do you have any temples on Nantucket, Andrew?" said Rosemary. "Shiva will be happy to visit them if you have any temples."

"I'm afraid we don't have any temples," said Andrew.

"The whaling museum," ventured Shiva. "The slaughter of majestic mammals."

"The courage of sailors," said Rosemary.

"Well, whatever it is, people tend to visit it," said Andrew.

"Visit what?" said Joe, turning to Sally.

"The whaling museum."

"Yeah, right," he said. "Gotta see the whaling museum. Lotta money in whaling once."

"Joe reduces everything to money," said Cynthia. "He turns reality into physics."

Andrew thought that was quite a witty comment, but no one was laughing.

"Or biology," said Joe a bit defensively.

"Or tax planning," said Shiva, which made *Joe* laugh. "But you are right, Cynthia. There are many ways of apprehending reality. You must take the right arrow from your quiver, depending on what beast you pursue."

"Do you hunt?" said Cynthia. "Joe's not much good with guns."

"I have shot a lot of birds," said Shiva. "Europeans like you to do that. Also deer." He paused, and it seemed to Andrew that he was studying Cynthia. How far a shot? What adjustment to make for the wind? There were so many ways the weekend could blow up. "In my youth," said Shiva, "I shot a tiger. Now it is forbidden."

"Oh, I would love to see a tiger. In the wild, I mean."

"That could be arranged," said Shiva. "Joe could come too. He would not need a gun."

Cynthia looked across the table at Joe. She seemed to Andrew, if only for a moment, like a child asking to go to the circus – asking with the same innocent air that made so many Americans want to watch her on television while they had breakfast, the same innocent air that made her a dangerous interviewer. It was all an act, Andrew realised.

"That's a handsome offer," said Joe.

Meaning, "we'll see," said Andrew to himself. Joe was eager for the deal. Letting Shiva entertain his wife was no problem, so long as he got the patents. He'd even go to India himself, if they did a deal. Closing party, maybe. Lotta money in India. That was how Joe's brain worked.

"Do you have your own jungle?" Cynthia asked Shiva.

"I think you could say that," said Rosemary, but Cynthia ignored her.

"We tend to call it a forest," said Shiva.

"With temples?" said Cynthia.

"Quite a few," said Shiva. He turned to Andrew. "But Prospero, my friend, I want to see all of your magical island."

Joe and Cynthia looked confused.

"Hero of Shakespeare's *The Tempest*," said Rosemary. "Shiva's unnaturally fond of Shakespeare."

"No, Rosemary," said Shiva, as if admonishing a child. "*Naturally* fond. How can anyone fail to love Shakespeare's plays?"

"Well, I've read them all, and some are distinctly better than others," said Rosemary.

"She's read them all," said Shiva, mimicking his wife. "And

she could write you a very good paper on *Hamlet*. But she does not *feel* them as I do."

"What he means," said Rosemary, "is that Shakespeare's characters are kings and princes, and that being a prince himself, Shiva responds to the plays in a visceral way, whereas Rosemary – being merely the daughter of an earl, and only the fourteenth of the title, making him a virtual parvenu – that poor Rosemary, despite her commendable mastery of the apparatus of scholarship, can never *really* appreciate the plays."

"Are you *really* a prince?" said Cynthia, cutting Rosemary off.

"I fear I am," said Shiva.

"Haven't you ever slept with a prince, Cynthia?" said Rosemary.

Cynthia ignored the question, but Joe responded: "She'll never tell, you know. She's a perpetual virgin – acts like every orgasm is a surprise."

A flicker of embarrassment crossed Cynthia's face. Sally came to her rescue. "I wish I could do that," she said.

"It gets old," said Joe. For a moment, no one spoke, and then Joe went on: "What I like, since we're talking about sex, and I suppose we should, Shiva – it's a way of getting acquainted when you think about it, a way of letting down your guard – what I like is a bit of struggle followed by enthusiastic participation. If a girl's got some...preferences, she ought to own up. If a man's got some preferences, the girl ought to figure out what they are. Don't you agree, Shiva? Andrew?"

"Would that life were so simple," said Shiva. "But let's talk about this later – man to man."

"Oh, please," said Rosemary.

A casual observer might have concluded, Andrew told

himself, that Shiva was way more sophisticated than Joe, that he was making fun of the American, even. But Andrew knew better. Someone who knew what Joe had accomplished as a businessman might have concluded that Joe was playing dumb to get Shiva to drop his guard. In Andrew's view, that wasn't true either. They each knew exactly what the other was doing. They were just warming up – like tennis players hitting balls back and forth before a match.

"Caliban," said Sally, as if on cue. "Andrew said you wanted to meet him, Shiva." Cathy must have told her that, Andrew realised; he didn't remember doing so himself

"See him," said Shiva. "I'd want to keep my distance. I have no need to *meet* a monster, which I think would mean *engaging* with him."

"One *engages* if the monster is inside oneself," said Andrew.

Rosemary turned and looked at him. "As it usually is," she said. It felt like she'd noticed him for the first time.

"I've never felt I had a monster inside me," said Joe.

"But you do," said Sally. "Everyone does."

"I don't," said Cynthia.

"Of course you do," said Rosemary. "Cathy is right. Everyone harbours a monster. Monsters are a culture's metaphorical representation of its desires and fears."

"And good sex," said Sally, "means bringing the monster out – talking to him, talking about him sometimes, parading him even."

"And you're good at that?" said Joe.

"Some people have thought so," said Sally, glancing at Andrew. "But going back to Caliban…"

"You're going to tell us that Moby Dick is Nantucket's Caliban," said Rosemary.

"Well, I wasn't," said Sally.

"But it's an interesting idea," said Andrew, responding to Rosemary. "The whale is certainly present in spirit…"

"I was going to say," said Sally, refusing to let Andrew divert the conversation, "that Caliban is pure sexual energy, which some cultures fear and some accept."

"Prospero," said Rosemary, "being a very wise man, has Caliban under his control. Shakespeare is saying that sex, like power, is what you make of it."

"Or what you let it make of you," said Sally.

"Ahab's obsession makes *him* a monster," said Andrew. "It makes him just as much a monster as the whale is. Obsession deforms us all, though some more than others." The thought briefly visited him that if obsession made monsters, the Governor of Massachusetts qualified. He'd been running for office since he was twelve.

There was also the thought that Sally had an agenda. Just what it was, Andrew couldn't say. But she'd clearly brought Caliban into the conversation in order to talk about sex – and to tease Andrew. She had to know he'd be wondering what would happen later that night.

"My obsession is my audience," said Cynthia. "I want to please them every single day, so they will tune in the next day. I don't think that makes me deformed."

"And it does not," said Shiva courteously.

"Lotta people think I'm obsessed with business," said Joe.

"I try not to be," said Shiva, "but sometimes I have no choice."

Sally started to clear away the salad plates. Andrew was going to have to figure her out. She knew *The Tempest*, which he would not have predicted. She believed in parading monsters.

Cynthia got up to help, which was also unexpected. Maybe there was something she wanted to say to Sally. Like, "Stay away from my husband." Joe was clearly intrigued.

Rosemary evidently didn't wait tables. With the others occupied in the kitchen, she was suddenly the only woman at a table with three men. It seemed to Andrew that she was somehow emphasising that point by being unnaturally still. It was impossible not to look at her. She could never be possessed, only desired. She accepted observation in the same way Andrew accepted Cathy's failure to give him as much sex as he wanted. Except that passivity made Rosemary beautiful and it made Andrew deformed.

"Does your wife go topless, Andrew?" Shiva said suddenly. "Or perhaps I should ask, what is the custom on magical Nantucket?"

Andrew didn't know how to answer. Cathy was a prude, but Sally clearly wasn't. He couldn't predict what she'd do.

"Lady Rosemary does not," Shiva continued, as if his wife weren't sitting there. "Doesn't even sunbathe. Wraps herself up in long sleeves and long trousers with a big floppy hat. You'll see tomorrow. She claims it has to do with her sensitivity to the sun, but I think it is pure selfishness. Someone as beautiful as Rosemary should be *required* to show herself from time to time."

Andrew had no idea where this was going. He didn't know what to do. He didn't like the idea of Rosemary being put on display, like Hester in *The Scarlet Letter*, as if her beauty were a crime. Hester hadn't had to disrobe, of course. It was Puritan New England. She'd just had to embroider a red "A" on her blouse. Perhaps Shiva had had something tattooed on Rosemary and that was why she kept covered up. What a horrible, fascinating idea.

Andrew's imagination changed religions and became a many-headed Hindu god. Shiva was a prince. Not that many generations ago, Lady Rosemary would have been his absolute possession, to do with as he wished. He came from a long line of men who had exercised such power. And women who had leapt on their husbands' funeral pyres. Rosemary's stillness was a reminder of that history. It was like a literary reference that gave depth and resonance to a text – only it was a gesture rather than words, and its impact was on Shiva and the life they shared. But was Rosemary's intention to give Shiva pleasure or to mock him? She did not strike Andrew as someone inclined to self-sacrifice.

Shiva began to laugh. For a moment Andrew thought the Indian had read his mind, but he seemed to be addressing Joe. "You said we should talk about sex as a way of becoming acquainted."

"Well, since you ask," said Joe, flustered for just a moment, "I don't know if Cyn goes topless. She never has when I've been around."

"Sin Goes Topless," Rosemary repeated. "Sounds like the title of an X-rated movie." The threat had gone out of the conversation, which was a relief. Or maybe it was Andrew's imagination that had calmed down.

"Yeah, funny about her name, isn't it?" said Joe.

"I think of her as 'Cynthia Jane,' of course," said Rosemary, but offered no further explanation.

Before Andrew could question her, Sally and Cynthia came in from the kitchen, carrying red and yellow plates of food. Cathy had gone to some trouble finding dinnerware that was both casual and beautiful – but not French provincial, which she insisted had become a cliché. "I thought leg of lamb tonight and lobster tomorrow," said the hostess.

"Sweetheart?" said Andrew. It felt quite daring calling Sally that. "Sweetheart, Shiva wants to know if this is a topless beach. I said I didn't know. There are so few houses at this end of the island."

"It's whatever we want it to be," said Sally, as if it were a question people often asked. "Personally, I find topless jolly. But I'll keep mine on if it troubles any of you." She set down three plates and went back towards the kitchen without waiting for a response.

"Cynthia?" said Shiva. It occurred to Andrew that the Indian was actually quite interested in the answer.

The glamorous Texan reached across the table and set down a lime-green bowl full of tossed salad. "You'll have to wait and see, won't you?" she said, not looking at him. She's decided innocent won't work, Andrew told himself.

"Wine, please, Andrew," said Sally. He got up and went to the sideboard, and then turned around to ask who was drinking what. Whoever was in charge of this party, it didn't feel like he was. It felt like losing control when he was first learning to ski. He'd never mastered skiing. Cathy was much better at it.

"Try the cabernet, Joe," said Sally.

"I believe I will," he said.

"Same for me, Andrew," said Sally.

"Same for all of us," said Rosemary, "and if Cyn and Shiva choose to leave it, that's their loss." She paused. "I like that for a movie title too: 'Sin and Shiva,' the Bollywood classic."

It occurred to Andrew that Rosemary was authorising her husband to have a little fun with Joe's wife. He had no idea whether that would be helpful or disastrous to his deal. You had

41

to accept that billionaires did that sort of thing. Andrew lived in a different world, even if he had visiting privileges.

There was a lot of passing glasses and distributing dinner plates and handing round the salad and the platter of lamb and roast potatoes. "Family style," said Sally. "It suits the beach."

"Yes," said Cynthia. "Imagine if we were a family – six sisters and brothers."

"We'd argue," said Shiva. Andrew recognised that as a reference to his disputes with his half-brothers. Joe had to get comfortable with the state of that litigation. He needed to arrange for the two of them to have a walk on the beach.

"If we were sisters and brothers," said Joe, "we wouldn't be allowed to fuck."

"What a pity that would be," said Sally, giving Andrew a sly look. We have a secret, her smile said. Secrets are sexy. And we don't *really* know where things are going. It occurred to Andrew that if he were the sort of man a lot of his business partners were, "intimacy without sex" would have a short half-life.

"So Cathy," said Joe, "how did you and Andrew meet?" Alarm bells went off in Andrew's head. Would Sally be able to make a history up for the two of them?

"We met in 1983," said Sally, which thankfully was correct.

"You sound like Philip Larkin," said Rosemary.

Andrew knew the reference but the rest of the table looked blank. "'Sexual intercourse began,'" he quoted, "'in 1963.'"

"'Which was rather late for me,'" Rosemary continued.

"'Between the end of the Chatterley ban,'" said Andrew.

"'And the Beatles' first LP,'" said Rosemary.

"That's actually a poem?" said Cynthia.

"Alleged to be," said Shiva. "I think it lacks grace and is more like a limerick."

42

"That's the point," said Rosemary.

"The point of what?" said Cynthia.

"I believe," said Shiva, "– correct me if I'm wrong, Rosemary – the grittiness of sex was one of Larkin's themes."

"Well, it began for me in Point Pleasant, on the Jersey shore, and I thought it was marvellous."

That was generous of Sally. Helpful, in fact. It never hurt to have a client think you were a stud. Andrew hadn't *felt* like a stud in quite a while, actually, but that wasn't the point. The point was what your clients believed – or even better, assumed without really thinking about it.

"I thought it was marvellous too," said Andrew. "My parents had a house at the shore. Cathy was working as a nanny, a few blocks away."

"He was pointed out to me," Sally continued. "He'd just graduated from Harvard. He was taking a few weeks of vacation before starting work at some super-prestigious firm on Wall Street. I was nineteen and about to be a sophomore at Smith. I wanted to meet him so I walked into him on the beach carrying three ice-cream cones."

"And offered to lick him off," said Rosemary.

"Not in so many words," said Sally.

"I asked her when she went off duty," said Andrew, which was true. Sally had said Cathy told her "everything," and perhaps she had. "We went to a movie."

"And afterwards we walked on the beach in the moonlight," said Sally. "The sand was still warm."

"I was unprepared," said Andrew.

"I said I didn't care. I was nineteen. I thought it was time I became a woman."

"A commendable attitude," said Shiva.

"We got married in August," said Sally, "and moved into a tiny apartment in Brooklyn. I never went back to Smith."

"And I've been working my ass off ever since," said Andrew, and was suddenly embarrassed. Telling billionaires how hard you've worked could sound like whining. For a moment no one said anything.

"So your daughter was conceived under the stars," said Shiva. "Does she know how beautiful that is?"

"I fear not," said Sally.

"Perhaps she'll come to see that as she gets older," said Shiva. "She's how old now?"

"Twenty."

"So you're what, Andrew? I assume you worked for a couple of years before business school."

"Forty-two," said Andrew. "I didn't go to business school. I went straight to work after college. I was in something called the 'analyst program' – a form of slave labour. If you did well enough, they made you an associate after three years." He felt like he was being interviewed for a job or considered for membership in a club.

"And partner nine years after that," said Joe, who as always had done his homework.

"Right," said Andrew, "except that the firm went public in the nineties, so we aren't really partners, even though we use the word."

"You look younger than forty-two," said Rosemary.

"Thank you – I guess," said Andrew.

"Were you a partner when the firm went public?" said Joe.

"Yes," said Andrew.

"So you made some money," said Joe.

"I was a pretty junior partner," said Andrew. "But yes."

"And all you've done since leaving college is crunch numbers and have ideas?" said Shiva.

"Pretty good ideas," said Joe.

"Not a bad life," said Shiva.

It would have been the moment for one of Andrew's guests to share some personal history, but the phone rang. "Probably a wrong number," said Andrew as he stood up and went into the kitchen. His heart was pounding.

It wasn't Cathy, or for that matter Eleanor. It was a man's voice. It was one of the infuriating men who ran the firm, newly named as head of investment banking and therefore theoretically Andrew's boss. "I've just been told you're not coming to the client outing tomorrow," said the man. "And what area code is this? I found the number on the phone list but it doesn't say. And your mobile phone must be turned off."

"Nantucket," said Andrew, "and no, I'm not." He realised he'd left his mobile upstairs.

"Could I ask why not?"

"I'm entertaining clients here."

"Well, it's very dislocating of you. I will have to rearrange the tennis. I wanted you and Cathy – that's your wife's name, right? – I wanted you to partner with the Ellises. We're trying to get his next equity offering – and damn it, what clients are you entertaining?"

Andrew named the men in the next room as quietly as he could.

"Can't hear you," said his new boss.

Andrew tried again.

"Right. But I wouldn't have called them *clients*. Do you even have a fee letter from either of them? That Indian has never signed a fee letter in his life, as I understand it."

"I need to get back to my guests," said Andrew evenly. And I need to figure out who is undermining me at work, he said to himself. There was always a price to pay for ignoring the politics.

"Oh, all right. But come see me Monday morning. I want to understand how you're spending your time. We have several things to talk about, as a matter of fact. We need to start running this place like a business."

"I won't be back in Manhattan until lunch time."

"Well, call my office and book a time then." He hung up.

Andrew took a few deep breaths and went back to the table, wrestling with the thought that the weekend would probably come to nothing. In the merger business, *most* good ideas died.

"Who was that, sweetie?" said Sally cheerfully, as if any news had to be good. She sounded like Cathy had ten years earlier.

"Fellow at the office," said Andrew. "Needed my advice on something."

"Did he really need it at nine on a Friday night?" said Rosemary. Her tone was both impatient and sympathetic.

"Evidently so," said Andrew.

"I think it's very nice that your partners want your help," said Shiva, which fortunately seemed to close the subject.

There was some clearing of plates and then the famous cheese course, as Cathy would have called it, which further confronted Andrew with the reality that his guests lived on Olympus and he was just a working stiff.

Sally brought in a wooden chopping board on which she had laid out the cheese, and a pile of crackers and lightly buttered toast points. She'd tied the shop's signature dark red ribbons around the board as a reminder of the luxury they were about to enjoy. "This is very spoiling," she said to Rosemary as she set it down.

"How did you manage, by the way?" said Cynthia. "I thought you said you'd just arrived from London. That was your Gulfstream we saw, right?"

"You flew from London to New York and then took the puddle-jumper back to Nantucket?" said Sally in amazement.

"Andrew told us he had tickets on the puddle-jumper," said Shiva grandly, "so we reported to the puddle-jumper. If that is the official way to come to your magical island, that is the way I wanted to do it."

"Like approaching a temple barefoot," said Cynthia.

"Precisely," said Shiva.

Andrew had always thought it quite grand to be able to give his guests tickets on the little plane from Manhattan. In the middle of the summer they were hard to come by, especially for the primo time slots like Friday evening. It had taken some wrangling with the airline, years ago, to convince them to issue blank tickets, and further argument, in the wake of 9-11, to get them to keep doing so.

"In answer to your question, Cynthia," Shiva continued, "Rosemary had the butler bring the cheese to the airport."

"You keep servants in New York," said Joe, "even though you live in London? I mean, I know you probably have an apartment here…"

"There's no point in having a flat if you don't have anyone looking after it," said Shiva. "I dislike the smell of a flat that no one is living in. You unlock the front door and stale air pours over you."

"And we travel at short notice sometimes," said Rosemary, as if that explained matters.

"A butler, a maid and a cook is all," said Shiva.

"We get such nice invitations," said Rosemary, smiling at Andrew.

4

Andrew came downstairs in the dark. He couldn't sleep. He'd had too much wine. He was terrified. He thought he should figure out how to call Cathy, even though she'd told him not to. Then again, he didn't much *want* to. That was probably why he'd left his mobile upstairs the previous evening. At some level, he wanted to run away as much as Cathy. He couldn't help feeling that was what she'd done.

He was angry about the call he'd gotten from his new boss. He didn't need to be *managed*. He certainly didn't need to be told he was wasting his time. His role, admittedly self-assigned, was to originate big "creative" deals – the sort that added to the firm's prestige as well as its bottom line. He decided what to work on. He didn't chew up a lot of associate resources, as some of his colleagues did, insisting on hundred-page presentations that said nothing new. His approach had paid off often enough so that he was entitled to patience and encouragement.

The weekend had started well, actually. His guests seemed to be enjoying themselves. They probably thought they were slumming and were letting themselves relax. Cynthia and Rosemary were never going to be friends, but they didn't have to be. Joe and Shiva were enjoying how different they were from each other. You could see it in the way they looked at each other.

Joe was *not* getting along with Cynthia, but that wasn't a crisis. Sally had explained the problem to him: Cynthia hadn't gotten used to not being the centre of attention, the way she was in her job. She hadn't been married to someone as rich as Joe before, or as single-minded. Come to think of it, she might not have been married before at all. Anyway, Cathy – correction, Sally – was going to buddy up with her the next day.

All that really needed to happen was for Joe and Shiva to have time to talk without any distractions. If a deal makes sense, Andrew often told himself, it will find a way to happen. He just *needed* this one to happen, that was all.

It was his own fault, of course. No one had insisted he chase big improbable deals. It was a choice he'd made – to live by his wits, as he put it to Cathy, rather than his elbows. He hadn't wanted to compete with his partners for ownership of the clients who rang the cash register on a regular basis – public utilities who issued debt every six months or conglomerates who shuffled prosaic subsidiaries with shameless frequency. There was a price to be paid for that cowardice: the randomness of success, and permanent anxiety. But if he couldn't deal with that, he didn't belong on Wall Street.

Andrew didn't turn on the kitchen lights because he knew about visual purple and he wanted to preserve his night vision. He did that on the mornings when he came downstairs before dawn and made a mug of coffee by feel and went out onto the porch to wait for the sky to lighten. "Beginning of morning nautical twilight," it was called: the point when you first could tell that sunrise was coming though it hadn't happened yet.

Some colleague who had served in the Navy had given him that phrase years ago. Andrew liked the way it suggested charts and remote places and the nineteenth century. He often wished he'd been in the Navy. His father would probably have liked that.

Sometimes he took his mug all the way to the beach, through the bushes and down the wooden stairway it had taken some persistence to be permitted to construct. There was rarely anyone on the beach at dawn, and he was occasionally tempted to set his mug down on the sand, take off his sandals, shorts and tee shirt and go into the water, but he knew better than to swim alone. The ocean is full of monsters, his father had taught him when he was four. At some level, he still believed that.

Presumably his father had seen it as a form of drown-proofing, a way of making an inquisitive toddler cautious during a vacation on the Jersey shore. His father had been a methodical and cautious man, who knew something about monsters, actually, but parents have no way of knowing which random comments their children will take to heart, what ideas will take root in their young imaginations. Andrew's younger daughter, Florence, for example, it had recently emerged, was studying architecture because he had once remarked that law school would be boring.

"You know, I would have made a pretty good lawyer," she'd said recently.

"Did you ever think about it?" he'd asked.

"You told me not to," she'd said.

Which wasn't what he'd meant at all. He'd never even gone to law school. How would he know? He'd meant that in his *observation*, lawyers needed an appetite for hard work, and that law school probably tested a person on that capacity.

"Oh," she'd said.

How else have I misled you? Andrew had said to himself.

"Never mind," she'd said. "I like architecture. Richard" –
that was the boy she thought she was in love with – "he told
me I pay attention to details the same as he has to. He says law
school has taught him to read. I told him drawing is teaching
me to see."

Which had brought the topic safely to a close. But still.

In any event, he always gave his house guests a lecture on
safety when they first arrived. And put a copy of *Moby Dick* in
every bedroom.

Andrew opened the refrigerator door to get a bottle of soda
water and…screw it. He wouldn't be able to see anything for
several minutes. He grabbed the bottle, closed the refrigerator
door and went into the pantry to get a glass.

There was someone in the pantry. A shape. A monster? He
slowly put down the bottle of soda water and reached out in the
darkness, finding…goosebumps, a woman's body, a shocking
frizz of curly hair, wetness beneath. "Oh my," he said, and
even as he said it realised his hand had stayed too long where it
shouldn't have been. "I beg your pardon."

Whoever went with the goosebumps grabbed the sleeves
of his nightshirt and pulled him toward her. "Relax," she
whispered. "What happens in the dark doesn't count."

"Why are you here?" he heard himself asking. "And
naked?"

"Why are you asking questions?"

Whispering didn't extinguish her accent. She had to be
Rosemary. His hands found her breasts, which were pushing
forward, eager for attention. "Do you even know who I am?"
she said.

Andrew told his hands to behave. "Of course I know. But what are you doing here? Who were you looking for?"

"I was looking for you. I wish you'd lose this nightshirt." She began pulling it up, and he resisted. "I want to go swimming," she said.

"It's dangerous at night. And how long have you been here?"

"It's not dangerous if I have a life guard. And the answer is I don't know, maybe half an hour. I was awake anyway. Shiva snores. Your other guests, the newlyweds, finished their duties hours ago. Very traditional couple, if you like that sort of thing."

What sort of thing, he wanted to ask, but didn't.

Rosemary paused, and changed her tone. "Listen, you're intelligent. You're on the edge of being middle-aged. Your wife is a bit distant, if I'm any judge, though superbly trained. It's three in the morning. Your profession involves sucking up to rich bastards. Wouldn't it balance things out if we went down to the beach and misbehaved?"

Andrew didn't answer.

"Well, at least *come* to the beach." She took his hand and led him out of the kitchen like the first girl he'd slept with, leading him down the hall of her parents' house one empty afternoon. In the silence he remembered what she looked like. The first girl he'd slept with, that is. He wished he hadn't stopped touching her breasts so soon. Now he was thinking of Rosemary.

When they got down the steps from the porch, she began to speak in a normal voice – normal in the sense of not being a whisper, but still aristo English intoxicating. "Do I need to tell you the terms of engagement?" she said. "Neither of us ever tells anyone what we've done."

"Is there anything particular you'd like?" Andrew said. He reminded himself that he was joking.

"If I tell you, it may not work," said Lady Rosemary. She evidently wasn't.

"Tell me why you do this then?" he said.

"You're right. I do this whenever I can – walk around someone else's house naked, that is. We get invited to a lot of very large houses. I do it to meet men. Sometimes it works. Now, where are those steps you mentioned that go down to the beach?"

"Through this little tunnel in the bushes." Now he was leading her.

"Oh, I like this little tunnel. It is dark in here. I love darkness. The man I'm with can't see me, and has to apprehend me with his other senses. Would you like to apprehend me a bit? I liked it when you touched me so rudely in the pantry and didn't know who I was."

Andrew felt it would be a mistake to touch her again. She touched his face. One of her fingers wandered into his mouth. He reached up and gently took her hand away.

"Hold my hand, then," she said. He led her through the tunnel and onto the steps, where there was a bit of a breeze, a bit of starlight.

"You're a beautiful woman," he found himself saying to her back as he followed her down the steps.

"If you want beauty," she said over her shoulder, "why won't you fuck me? I will become your fantasies." There was a hint of sadness in her question, uninhibited as it was. A suggestion of struggle. It reminded him of Sally's "intimacy without sex" – though perhaps the other way round. Sally who was an unexploded bomb asleep in his bed.

"Because you're a goddess and I'm a mortal," said Andrew in answer to Rosemary's question. There was a point to the Greek and Latin he had studied after all. "Because your husband is a prince."

"I *thought* you might be a poet," said Rosemary matter-of-factly, starting down the beach. "You certainly have a lot of poetry stuffed in your head, same as me. So you will understand. The fates played a cruel trick on me. I am beautiful, as you say. I say that without embarrassment or conceit because it is not something I achieved or earned."

"Not like your first-class honours."

"Thank you for knowing about that," she said. "Take my hand, please. At least that, as we walk."

Andrew did so. What a picture we make, he said to himself: naked Venus with a middle-aged investment banker in a red-and-white striped nightshirt, which billows when the breeze catches it. Well, almost middle-aged, he corrected himself. His curly black hair hadn't retreated yet. He was fitter than he deserved to be, considering how little formal exercise he got.

"I had to work hard for my first," Rosemary was saying, "though of course the brains that made it possible were also an unearned gift. But my beauty is just...there. I eat what I like, exercise or not as I choose, wear what I feel comfortable in. Here's an experiment I tried. I went out to lunch in London in a really ugly outfit. No jewellery. No make-up. Fancy restaurant. The paparazzi spotted me. Next morning one of the tabloids had a spread, claiming this was the newest fashion trend. And, here's what's awful: I looked really good."

"I'm not sure you have a complaint, my lady."

"Let me continue. Along with my looks, I have an enormous sex drive. I want it twice a day, really."

"Lucky Shiva."

"Lucky you, if you'd just cooperate. I like sleeping with Shiva's professional advisers – which I take it is what you're trying to be. I go after you lawyer and banker chappies because you have a strong interest in keeping the liaison a secret. In case you're interested." They walked on in silence for a bit. "Also, it's a way of disrespecting him, fucking his servants. And meaning no disrespect to you, sweet Andrew." It occurred to Andrew that he was safe, at least for now. The intoxication had waned. She was crazy.

"Shiva is perverse," she continued. "He thinks I desire him. He likes thinking that. He maintains it intensifies his pleasure to have me less often than I'd like. He's told me all this. 'A beautiful wife is a treasure,' he says. 'A wife overflowing with desire is a magical possession.' He thinks that my being horny makes him smarter. He wants me to be Miranda at the start of the play. That's why he goes on about *The Tempest*. 'O brave new world that has such creatures in it.' You know that scene, I assume, where Prospero's daughter, having been raised on an island with no men except her father, sees the shipwrecked Ferdinand. Shiva likes that moment, where Miranda's desire is awakened but not yet fulfilled. He believes – and I promise you there is nothing to support this in the text – he believes that keeping Miranda pure is what makes Prospero strong. Shiva thinks he's Prospero, of course."

"So why does he call *me* that?"

"He's being polite. It's your island. And he's giving you a hint. Find a way to tell him he's the magician. He will like that."

"That's very helpful."

"But to go on, the other bit of irony the fates hung around

my neck like a golden chain is that my beauty frightens most men. I go out to dinner and the boy beside me becomes tongue-tied. I let my dressing gown fall to the floor and so does his erection."

Andrew laughed. "Surely not."

"More often than you'd think. Even at university."

"But you don't need lots of lovers. You just need a husband who likes sex as much as you do. I hesitate to say this. I am supposed to be winning Shiva's trust. But have you considered looking for such a person?"

"Every day. But you know, being rich is addictive. I would get very little in a divorce. I have no grounds. Or none I care to talk about in public. You will understand this, Andrew, being a poet. I'm Prometheus's unmentioned sister. The eagle of sexual hunger tears at me every night." They walked in silence for a bit, and she played with his hand. "But when I do find a man who appreciates the gift of my fire, the pleasure for both of us is intense."

"That was beautiful," said Andrew. And then: "We should probably go back."

"All right," said Rosemary, letting go of Andrew's hand and turning towards him. "But for my pains, one kiss?"

It was a very good kiss.

Andrew had one more question for her, though. "Why did you marry Shiva?"

"I thought I was being clever. One wants to keep on being clever when one has gotten a first. The fact that my parents objected was a further inducement of course."

Neither of them spoke for a while, but when they entered the tunnel through the shrubbery, she grabbed his nightshirt again and pulled him to her. "I want to use the darkness again.

Just touch me somewhere." He let his hands find her breasts. "You are very brave," she said. "Whatever happened on that phone call, you managed to lock it up. Don't worry. You looked fine. But I could tell. If you're married to a man like Shiva, you see a lot of supplicants. I know what suppressed fear looks like in a man. And I like you, sweet Andrew, who took me to the beach but wouldn't take advantage of me. I think I'm going to like you very much. Whatever it is you're trying to accomplish here, I'll help you if I can. I never pay attention to the business aspects of our existence, you realise. Shiva's and my existence, that is. All the nice invitations."

"I want your husband and Joe to merge overlapping bits of their respective empires," and Andrew.

"So they need to become friends," she said, "at least for a while?"

Andrew took a deep breath. "Yes," he said. He certainly hoped they would. "Quite a while," he added.

When they got to the house, Andrew told Rosemary to go up to her room. He'd wait on the porch for a while. She was back within seconds, however. "Shiva's not there," she said.

"Does he know about your night-time prowling?"

"He knows about my *insomnia*. I'll just slip back into bed, and be asleep when he returns from whatever he is doing. He must be trying to seduce your wife, by the way, because I hear voices coming from your room. I would recommend you not confront him."

"I will go into the maid's room at the end of the pantry," said Andrew, not sure he should have agreed so readily. "I'll pretend I snore. He does that too, I think you said."

"A good listener and a wise banker," said Rosemary. And kissing him lightly on the cheek, she scampered upstairs again.

5

Andrew woke up in the maid's room. It took him a moment to remember where he was. Thick curtains covered the windows but there was bright sunlight at the edges. Something had happened in the middle of the night, but he couldn't let himself get distracted remembering it. He had a weekend to manage.

Feeling foolish in his red-and-white striped nightshirt, he hurried through the pantry to the kitchen, saw the remnants of several breakfasts, began to panic. His watch and mobile phone were upstairs, he thought, but from the brightness of the sun it could be after nine. The house was quiet. What if everyone had left? Shiva could have sent for his plane. Joe could have chartered a boat. Sally could have quit.

He looked into the living room. Rosemary was sitting on the sofa, reading. That was a relief. It was very nice, in fact. Looking at her was like eating honey. She was wearing linen long pants and a matching long-sleeve blouse. The colour was hard to name: faded apricot? It complemented her white-blonde hair. Her hair was a mess – and perfect. She was what had happened in the middle of the night.

"You're awake," she said, looking up from her book. "Come sit next to me."

He did, leaving space between them.

"I've sent Joe and Shiva walking to the lighthouse, which should take them a couple of hours. I told Shiva he could regard a lighthouse as a kind of temple. Joe took his map. He's a bit nutty about maps."

Ah.

"The girls have gone for a run in the opposite direction, so as not to be in the way. Cathy made sure of that. She's good. I expect they'll get into the water before they come back. Cathy went to town early and bought muffins and lobsters. Stay put. I'll get you one – a muffin, that is – and how do you like your coffee?"

"Black. No sugar."

"Oh, and good morning," she said. She leaned across the space he had left between them and kissed him on the mouth.

"Indeed," said Andrew, blinking. The kiss had been more than perfunctory. "You didn't want to go out?"

"I don't do sunshine, remember. And I would have been a fifth wheel. Or a third wheel. And think how you'd have felt if you'd woken to an empty house."

"I thought I had."

"Don't talk until you've had some coffee." She went into the kitchen. So maybe he didn't have to manage the weekend. Why had he felt so frightened?

Rosemary brought his breakfast and sat down next to him again, but closer. She spread a napkin on his lap and broke off a piece of the muffin. "Let me feed you," she said. "Butter?"

"Please. I think I'd better hold the mug myself, though."

"As you like." She popped a bite of buttered muffin into his mouth, and prepared another one while he chewed. "This way I can keep you from talking. I don't want you saying anything foolish. It could make you foolish all day."

"Mmmm," said Andrew. Food was good. Was it only Saturday?

"Shiva wasn't trying to seduce your wife, I'm pleased to report. He was in the bathroom. The person in your bedroom was Joe. He'd knocked on your door because Cynthia needed an aspirin. Finding Cathy alone, he talked to her for a bit, which must have been a bore for Cynthia. That's their story, anyway, and they're sticking to it."

"Mmmm."

"My story is that I couldn't sleep so I went and sat on the porch. My home time zone is London, remember."

"And what's my story?"

"You snore. Cathy's a light sleeper, she says. There's something wrong about her that I haven't figured out, but she's playing along." Rosemary buttered another piece of muffin and put it in Andrew's mouth. Her fingers were long and cold.

"Playing along with what?" said Andrew, his mouth still full of muffin.

"I told you not to talk," said Rosemary. "Just listen.'

She reminded him of Sally at the airport. All the women in his life were doing things for him except Cathy. Even Eleanor had opened a door, if inadvertently.

"Shiva is genuinely interested in your deal or we wouldn't be here. I should have told you that last night. The person you need to focus on is Joe. He strikes me as a control freak. He could get on Shiva's nerves."

The coffee was beginning to do its job. Rationality returned. "I think I must have had a nightmare," said Andrew.

"Oh, thank you very much," said Rosemary.

"No, sorry, that part was nice. Hard to believe. Spectacular. I've never encountered a goddess before. What I meant about a nightmare is, I'm abnormally anxious this morning. Don't know why. Have to get over it. Comes with the job." He had lots of reasons to be anxious, actually, including the fact that his wife had gone missing and the lurking suspicion that he was relieved. He couldn't tell Rosemary that, though to be honest he half wanted to. "Why did you think your husband was seducing Cathy?" he asked her, trying to take control of the conversation.

"He does that sort of thing sometimes. He thinks it puts me in my place."

"And you don't?"

"Oh, I throw myself at men occasionally. I told you that last night. But we can discuss ethics later. What we need now is a strategy. Here's my plan. We have at least an hour, probably an hour and a half. You need some horizontal therapy. You will not be able to manage these monsters if you are afraid. The only answer to your anxiety is sex. Fortunately for you, I like sex – as I've told you. Go to the maid's room and undress. There's a shower in there, right? I will bring you clean clothes for afterwards."

She left her copy of *Moby Dick* on the sofa. She turned and smiled at him just before she went up the stairs. Do as you're told was what the smile said. So much for taking control. If they were going to have an argument, perhaps it was better to do it in the maid's room. He got up and went there, carrying his mug and breakfast dishes to the kitchen on the way. He decided to undress. She seemed so certain that was the right next move.

"You were in a very bad way," she said afterwards. "Better?"

"Thank you," he said, "I think." He had just broken a cardinal rule of his previous existence. It didn't feel bad yet.

"Think about this," she said, turning towards him and letting him contemplate her breasts, "and I apologise for rushing things. If I am not on your side, if I made love to you for sport, if you're going to regret it, you will see it in my face in the next minute. I will cough and pull away by a few centimetres. My smile will congeal. I will make a joke. Now, look at me. Is any of that happening?"

Andrew studied her for the full minute. "No," he said. "But are you sure you're not a sorceress?"

"Of course I'm a sorceress. And on this magical island, my powers are increased. I can make my husband fall in love with Joe – as a business matter, that is – so long as you believe in me. And by the way, I think you need an ally."

"Do I have a choice?"

"Not really."

"Then I'd better tell you everything."

"That would be wise."

"Cathy isn't Cathy. She's the au pair. My wife has disappeared."

"You are braver than I thought."

"What about the au pair? She's pretty brave too, don't you think? Her real name is Sally by the way."

"She's a good actress, but I'm not sure that qualifies as bravery. She has nothing to lose. How long has she worked for you?"

"A bit more than a week."

"She must like having a new wardrobe."

"Yes, and I find it quite spooky."

"It's a magical island," said Rosemary.

"Will Sally know you know she's not Cathy?" Andrew asked.

"Not unless you tell her. You'll have to get back in bed with her tonight, you realise. I take it you two aren't having sex. But why did you decide to pretend she was Cathy?"

"It was her idea. She offered it as a solution. I had to make the decision quickly. I thought you might be offended that Cathy wasn't here when you'd come all the way from London."

"Well, I might have been. I get difficult when I'm bored. But this is much more interesting. And now that I have a crush on my host, I hope his wife never reappears." Rosemary paused and scratched her shoulder. "I'm wondering why pretend Cathy hasn't insisted you fuck her, though. You wouldn't have a choice."

"Maybe she doesn't fancy me."

"She's not the sort of woman who would let that stand in her way. She must have other plans."

"She's quite a good tease." Andrew explained about intimacy without sex.

"Oh, I expect Sally has many talents. But your wife is terrible."

Andrew started to come to Cathy's defence, but decided it would be too much trouble.

Joe and Shiva returned as predicted, half an hour after Andrew had shaved and showered and dressed. They sat on the porch sweating and pouring sand out of their shoes. Rosemary brought them both bottled water. "We have beer too," she said to Joe, "but I'll need a note from your parents."

"I'll follow Shiva's example," he said.

"Good plan," said Rosemary.

Sally and Cynthia appeared fifteen minutes later, in

64

running shorts and shoes, but having stuffed their sports bras into their pockets. "It is now officially a topless beach," said Sally.

"She dared me," said Cynthia. She sat down next to Shiva. She alternated between turning this way and that to show off, and covering herself with her hands. It was amusing to watch, actually. Andrew doubted she fully realised what she was doing.

"For a woman who's had two children, Cathy," Rosemary said to Sally, "your breasts are very nice."

"Thank you," said Sally. "There are benefits to being flat-chested."

"I wouldn't say she's flat-chested," said Cynthia reflexively and then looked embarrassed.

"Are you going to give us a point of comparison, Rosemary?" said Shiva.

"No," said his wife. "I'm going to start making lunch, so you all can take showers." She stood up. "Come help me, Andrew."

"It's all in plastic cartons in the refrigerator," said Sally. "You might take out what's left of the cheese. There are baguettes I bought this morning in a paper sack in the pantry. But I should be doing all that."

Rosemary turned around. She'd started to roll up her sleeves. "You should be doing exactly what you're doing now," she said quietly, speaking to herself, really. "Giving the men a treat, and giving Cynthia an excuse to do the same."

Andrew followed Rosemary into the kitchen. "This is good," she said. "Is there something we can discover we need to go get in town? I want to leave the four of them alone."

"I don't think there's enough cheese, probably. And maybe we need more sparkling water. We didn't count on there being two non-drinkers."

"Grab your keys," said Rosemary. "Short errand," she called out. They were out the door before anyone could object.

"Can you tell me what we're doing?" Andrew said once they were on the road to town.

"Male bonding," said Rosemary. "Joe and my royal husband are going whoring together."

"What?"

"Even if nothing happens, the situation will be something they share. Cynthia is attracted to my husband – to the extent she knows how to do that. She has her reasons. He's exotic. She has probably never been with a brown person. Shiva enjoys the fact that she's fascinated. He's been giving blonde English girls a bit of excitement since he was sixteen. Didn't you see him watching her as she displayed? It reminded me of that David Attenborough film with gannets courting: bill up, bill down, touch necks, ruffle tail feathers. Joe, very conveniently, is fixated on your Sally-Cathy person. And he's getting rather tired of Princess Cynthia. I give that marriage less than a year."

"You can see all that?" said Andrew. Rosemary didn't answer. They drove in silence for a few minutes. "So we're leaving them alone to misbehave," said Andrew. "You like that word, as I recall."

"We're leaving them alone to let them think about it. Which they will. Your au pair knows her job."

"Which is?"

"As I said, she's helping Princess Cynthia be less inhibited. I'll bet you a long wet kiss Sally-Cathy manages to get into the shower and then remember something she needs downstairs and accidentally gets seen and then shrugs it off, setting an example for Mrs Joe."

"How do you know that?"

"I've done it myself, my sweet. Anyway, the crucial question is, will Princess Cynthia offer herself to my husband. He'd like that. He likes it when he can seduce a woman just by existing."

"And the fact that she's married to his prospective business partner is of no consequence?"

"Oh, it's of every consequence. Remember, Shiva is a prince. The rules for him are different. If Joe lets him have his wife, that makes Joe his vassal, which means he can allow Joe to make more of the *business* decisions, which is what Joe cares about. They don't talk about it as such, of course. It has to just happen – like dripping wet Sally-Cathy getting surprised in the kitchen."

"She's supposed to be my wife, remember. Should I care whether Joe fucks her?"

"Of course you should care – officially – but you never say a word about it. Pay attention to the other cars, please."

"Sorry. Death wish, I suppose."

"Don't be stupid."

"So in this psychodrama you're describing, what am I supposed to do?"

"You're supposed to have the hots for me, which Sally-Cathy can see, which gives her the moral right to flirt with Joe. I'm not sure if they should go to bed or not. I'm not sure if anyone should get to consummate their fascination – except us, of course. Sally-Cathy flirting with Joe will get you a bigger fee, by the way, but we won't talk about that because it's disgusting. What is your fee, by the way?"

"Twenty million – ten from each of them. But I haven't raised the subject yet."

"Don't. The main thing is that Joe stops caring what

Princess Cynthia does, giving her permission to stroke Shiva's ego, at least until you collect your fee. Can you get a couple of lawyers out here tomorrow?"

"You're kidding?"

"Watch me."

When they got back with the cheese and bottled water, Rosemary instructed Andrew to find Shiva and talk to him. "See what he thought of Joe. I can find out what Joe thought, but the one thing I cannot do is talk business with Shiva."

"Why not?"

"I'm supposed to be an aristocrat, and therefore completely uninterested in the subject."

"So…ah…how was the lighthouse?" said Andrew, sitting on the porch with Shiva as Sally and Rosemary set the table.

"Too far away." Most guests thought that – which was why they were sent to see it.

"I thought you said you got there," said Andrew.

"We did. And walked up the hundred and fifty stone steps. And walked back quite briskly. That's why I'm exhausted. I live in London. I have a driver. I rarely walk anywhere – and certainly not on loose sand."

"I would have said something before you set out, only I was asleep."

"I expect I will live," said Shiva. "Also I learned something important about your friend Joe."

"He's not my friend any more than yours," said Andrew. This was technically correct, though he found the American easier to talk to. "What did you learn?"

"He has a lot of energy. I suppose that's why he needs a new wife every few years. He uses them up. But more to the point, Joe *loves* doing business. He likes it so much, he's honest.

Cheating a customer or a supplier would be a distraction from the pleasure of simply *doing* the deals, building a better mousetrap, capturing market share, *dominating* the market, all the while watching the way the stars and planets are moving, and shifting focus eighteen months ahead of the competition. He's done that trick three times now, you realise, changed gears before his competitors knew they needed to. He's almost supernaturally talented."

"Be fair to yourself," said Andrew. "People say you're a visionary too." And remembering Rosemary's advice, he added. "The *Financial Times* called you a 'magician.'"

"That was kind of them, wasn't it," said the Indian. "But the problem is, Andrew, I cannot any longer do all the things I think of doing, the things I wish to do. I barely do the things I am *required* to do.

"I'm fifty-two. That isn't old, but it isn't young. I had a strenuous youth. I played polo – if you can believe it, looking at me now. I was fairly good at it. That and my family's name opened a lot of doors. I pursued movie stars. I lost money in casinos. For a while, I lived a glamorous life. Then, inconveniently, my father died and I had to become responsible. In order to appear mature, I started reading – always a dangerous habit – I stopped gambling, made new friends, realised that a man in my position cannot have friends, stopped drinking, studied finance. I had to do that last bit in secret, you understand. A magician is supposed to just...*know* things."

"Prospero had his books," said Andrew, "which he studied."

"You must have been talking to Rosemary," said Shiva.

"Why do you say that?"

"You *called me* Prospero. She knows I like that. But never mind. The point is that I have been on stage for a very long time.

A vast audience watches me. India watches me. Hundreds of thousands of employees depend on me. That sort of attention is difficult to sustain.

"I have a strenuous family. Children by an earlier wife. One needs heirs, and they have to be brown, I think. Nice boys, whom I do not know as well as I should. I can only hope they do not turn out like my brothers. Half-brothers, that is, by my father's subsequent wives.

"And then of course there is Rosemary. Who has read all of Shakespeare. Who is fifteen years younger than I am. Whom I cannot fully satisfy – to my great regret. She is definitely strenuous."

Andrew was of course desperate to ask Shiva whether he and Joe could be partners. But he didn't. People tell you things when they are ready to, he'd found.

6

Lunch was strenuous too. The landline rang right after they'd all sat down. Andrew hurried into the kitchen, feeling sick. Four hours earlier he'd been unfaithful to Cathy for the first time in his marriage, and now she was calling to tell him about Eleanor. Their daughter was probably fine, and telling Cathy she needn't have come, but his wife would need reassurance, and perhaps advice. He wouldn't be able to provide it. He couldn't afford to be away from the table very long. He mustn't be overheard. He couldn't stop thinking about Rosemary's perfect body.

It wasn't Cathy. It was the Governor of Massachusetts. "Andrew, my old friend, I need your help." They *were* old friends, actually. They had vomited on the same Cambridge sidewalks when they were freshmen. They'd witnessed each other's failures. "I'm here on Nantucket and it turns out Lydia is getting back from California a week early. She thinks her mother is dying. She probably *is* dying. We all are, if you think about it. But the old bird is taking her time about it. She told Lydia to go back to the East Coast. She says it's ghoulish of her children to sit around waiting for her to die.

So Lydia will be here in a few hours."

"That all sounds like good news," said Andrew hopefully.

"Well, in theory it is. But I'd brought someone to the house for the weekend."

"A female someone?"

"Two of them, actually, which I'd hoped would be less incriminating. They're on my staff. Smart girls. Hard workers. Bit of a reward."

"They wouldn't by any chance happen to be gorgeous?"

"One of them is. Well, probably both. Judy is certainly attractive. I just can't think of her that way. Small and dark – Italian mother – very smart and very sweet. Too intense for me. I prefer Janis. She's the red-head. But I haven't, you know…I'm too old for that. I just like people to think I'm not. So anyway, I need a place to stash them. If Cathy would be prepared to invite them to stay it would avoid unpleasantness. Lydia sounds pretty strung out from dealing with her mother. She doesn't need any long explanations. Never been good at them. You have a lot of bedrooms, as I remember it."

"Some of them are occupied this weekend."

"Perfect. It will look like they're friends of your daughters."

"Uh…"

"Thanks, Andrew. I'll bring them over in the next two hours."

The Governor of Massachusetts hung up. Andrew stared at the receiver for a moment and then replaced it in the cradle. George always got what he wanted. If you were going to be his friend, you had to accept that. Or his wife, Andrew supposed. If you were going to be his wife, that is. Or his mistress.

George might or might not have stopped fooling around, but there had always been plenty of candidates for his attention.

"I'm interviewing a new applicant," was the way he'd put it when they were undergraduates and he was taking a girl to New York. "Sex is better out of town," he claimed. "You fly down from Boston. You act really cool on the plane – like it was an accident you were sitting next to each other. You tell her that's in case you run into somebody one of you knows. You check into your hotel but then right away you go out to lunch, walk in Central Park, maybe visit a museum, let the afternoon trickle away. And all the time there's this double bed waiting for you in the hotel, which she can't stop thinking about…"

Andrew had just gotten back to the table when his mobile phone rang. He'd finally remembered to put it in his pocket. He apologised to his guests and went into the kitchen to talk. It was a man's voice, but not George. "Andrew?"

"Yes."

"Peter here. Where are you?"

"Nantucket."

"Ah. Look, I just happened to be in the office to get some papers, and – I won't beat around the bush – did you know they're moving your office?"

Andrew didn't reply.

"I'll take that for a 'no.' You don't need to answer. Anyway, they are. We evidently need more conference rooms. A few of us are moving to twenty-six. A kick in the balls, of course, but it's not a bad set-up. I was told Thursday, so I've told them how I want the furniture arranged. The offices are almost the same size, but there isn't room for all my pictures. I talked to the guys who are doing the moving. Did you realise there are people whose entire career consists of moving bankers to different offices whenever they reorganise us here? Anyway, they said, quote, 'we ain't got no instructions about this other office.' So unless you talk to them right away, when you come in Monday, your new office is going to look like you're holding a garage sale." He paused. "Sorry. You were probably having a nice weekend out on Nantucket. I thought you'd be at the outing, actually. I liked it when you had Mary and me to Nantucket for the weekend one time. Anyway, I thought you'd want to know. I'll text you the guy's mobile number, the one who's running the move."

"Thanks." What shits. He'd been in the office on Thursday and most of Friday. They could have told him about the move. And he and Cathy were supposed to be charming the Ellises while it was happening.

Andrew went back to the dining room. He couldn't possibly deal with the men who spent their lives moving bankers from floor to floor. He didn't know what to say to his guests, so he didn't say anything. He tried eating but the food had no flavour. It was possible he needed to throw up.

"Business?" said Rosemary.

"It isn't usually this bad," said Sally.

"Nice to be wanted," said Shiva.

"I suppose," said Andrew.

The land line rang again. Andrew went back to the kitchen. *This* would probably be Cathy. It was the Governor. "Listen, I've got to bring them over right now. Lydia caught an earlier plane. Please apologise to Cathy, but I won't even have time to come in." That at least would be helpful.

Andrew went back to the dining room. "Small change of plans," he said.

To be honest, it suddenly felt like a major change of plans. Or a change in the weather. If he'd been in a conference room, doing a deal, he could have said exactly what difference it made to have someone new at the table. He would have known what to say to his client, what to warn him about, what *quid quo pro* to suggest. But he wasn't playing for money, he was playing for his life, which can make it harder to see matters clearly. He wouldn't have said that a moment earlier – the melodramatic bit about playing for his life, that is – but the phrase having come into his head, he thought it had validity. His old friend George represented youthful dreams. When such ghosts come on stage in an opera, the music changes.

"It shouldn't be a problem," he continued, "but we have some more people staying. My friend George is a bit overcommitted socially. We have extra bedrooms. I haven't met the young women but he says they're well brought-up."

Shiva began to laugh. "You're talking about the Governor?"

"We went to school together. We're friends. That is, if politicians have friends."

"Can I help you make beds?' said Rosemary to Sally.

"Let's find out what the, ah, sleeping arrangements will be first," said Sally. "There's one more proper bedroom and then a bunk room that can take eight."

"We could *all* sleep there," said Shiva. He seemed to find the situation amusing. "It would be like summer camp. I went to a summer camp in Maine when my uncle was at the United Nations. Eight little boys per cabin."

"Who are these people who are crashing our party?" said Cynthia. She was evidently not amused. Interesting that she thought it was her party. Rosemary would probably tell him that Cynthia thought every party was about her. "Are we talking quote interns here, or full-fledged bimbos?" said Cynthia. "Do we let them join us for dinner?"

"We're going to need more food," said Sally.

"They work for the Governor," said Andrew. "He's a political rock star – as you would know, Cynthia. You'll probably find they're former Supreme Court clerks."

"Look, I actually know the Governor," said Cynthia. "He has a bit of a reputation."

"Agreed," said Andrew, standing up. It occurred to him that perhaps Cynthia was feeling uncomfortable about having shed her top earlier, and in unconscious reaction was turning prudish. Or maybe she and the Governor had some history.

All those trips to New York. And if a girl was a "finalist," as he put it, he'd take her to Nantucket in the off season. His family had a house, which had passed to George. "Nantucket in late autumn is extremely out of town," he liked to say. "You go for a walk on the beach, you come in and light the fire. They usually like the house."

What he meant about the house was that it was rather grand, and reminded an "applicant" that George came from a very old family, which it would be comfortable and gratifying to be part of. Not that he planned to give her membership.

"So much more reason to be polite to these young women," said Rosemary, briefly interrupting Andrew's reverie.

George seemed to specialise in girls who *weren't* named "Cabot" or "Adams," or something equally famous, but definitely knew what those names meant. Andrew had pointed this out to him once. They were good enough friends for him to do so.

"Of course I do," George had said. "If you want to get what you want, Andrew, you need to use every bit of leverage you have." They were both nineteen then, and Andrew was still a virgin.

"I suppose that's how politicians think," Andrew had said.

They both knew George planned to run for Congress as soon as he could.

Whatever the reason, Cynthia seemed to find the prospective intrusion of these two young women who worked for the Governor annoying. "Supreme Court clerks, my ass," she said. Perhaps what bothered Cynthia wasn't propriety but simply the introduction of new variables into the situation. She wanted to be in control and this would make it harder.

Andrew watched Rosemary watching Cynthia, and Shiva watching them both. He finds them amusing, Andrew said to himself, but not necessarily desirable. What in the world do I do about that? Do I need to do anything?

"Andrew," said Shiva, standing up, "let me be helpful. If you'll give me the keys to your car, Cynthia and I will go buy some more lobsters."

"The lobster man has probably run out by now," said Sally.

"Steaks, then," said Shiva.

"I thought you people didn't eat beef," said Joe.

"I don't, and if Andrew's surprise visitors are my co-religionists, we have a provisions problem." Shiva interrupted himself with an undignified giggle. "But if I know anything about the Governor, these orphans he is depositing on our doorstep will have long legs, blue eyes and American passports. So steak it is."

"How do you know the Governor of Massachusetts?" said Joe.

"I met all kinds of people when I was a younger man," said Shiva. "We had a few narrow escapes together."

"Why do I have to go buy groceries for people we don't even know?" said Cynthia.

"I do it all the time," said Sally, and then covered her

mouth in mock embarrassment. Andrew didn't think Cynthia had heard her, which was fortunate. He supposed Sally was trying to cheer him up. She'd clearly amused Shiva, who laughed briefly and then went deadpan.

"Narrow escapes" was another of George's expressions. It meant "I thought I was in love but I came to my senses," or "Her mother had plans," or "For a week there, it looked like she was pregnant."

Andrew had missed the year George grew up. They were in their mid-twenties. He and Cathy were living in Brooklyn with baby Eleanor. There wasn't any money. George was going to law school and as he put it later, "working hard for the first time." He'd evidently gotten a girl pregnant. She wasn't a typical "applicant." He'd "lost focus," as he put it. He'd wanted her to get an abortion. She wouldn't. But she wouldn't tell her parents who the father was, either. And she wouldn't take any money.

"So there was this woman with your child, somewhere in Boston, giving you a guilty conscience," Andrew had said to him when he confessed years later.

"There still is," George had said.

"And you married Lydia as penance," said Andrew.

"That's the way it turned out."

George had missed the "go and sin no more" part, but he'd done well in law school, let Lydia's mother throw a net over him the following summer, when he did an internship in Los Angeles – "my California experiment ," he called it – and after graduation brought his bride back to his ancestral city.

Andrew and Cathy hadn't been able to afford the air fare to attend the wedding, but were forgiven. "It was a bit plastic," George reported.

Sally took the keys off the nail in the kitchen and handed

them to Shiva, mouthing "thank you," but before he could get Cynthia out the door, the Governor arrived, handed over his orphans and made his getaway. Judy and Janis stood blinking on the porch. Definitely new music.

"Please come in, and have you had lunch?" said Sally.

They had not.

"Which one of you is which?" said Andrew, rallying at the sight of two more good-looking women.

"I'm the red-head," said Janis, which earned her a laugh from the men. And yes, long legs. She extended her hand to Joe. He introduced himself. "But you're a billionaire," she said. "You have more money than God, and I'm about to have lunch with you. Gosh."

"Only if you have good table manners," said Rosemary, as if it were a joke the red-head was already in on. There was something about Janis that told you she would know which fork to use. It was clear she knew how to handle men.

Andrew studied her covertly. Rosemary was evidently prepared to like her, which made her interesting. Her face and arms and calves were dusted with freckles. You'd have to say she was pretty, though the headline was competence. She was wearing navy blue shorts and a matching polo shirt, looked fit, might have been an athlete once, would undress in front of a man without embarrassment. For half a moment, it occurred to Andrew that there would be vulnerabilities in there too, but the thought disappeared before he could examine it. Anyway, how would he know what went on in this stranger's head?

"I'm Shiva," said Shiva.

"He *is* God," said Joe.

"Nice to meet you, God," said Janis.

More laughter. Sally began to pull extra chairs up to

the table. Everyone sat down. Fresh plates were issued. Food was passed. Cynthia came into the room. She'd been in the bathroom fixing her lipstick or something. Andrew was losing track. "Just to get things straight," she said without introduction, "is either of you a Supreme Court clerk?"

"She was," said Janis. "I'm the dumb one. And I know who you are."

Cynthia gave Janis a smile. She liked being recognised, Andrew realised.

"But you've actually practised," said Judy, responding to Janis. She mentioned the name of a prominent firm in New York, where Janis had presumably worked, but no one was paying attention to her, which didn't seem to bother Judy at all. "She's heaps older than me, too," Judy added. She was shorter than Janis, had smooth olive skin, longish black hair and a decent figure, but what drew your attention were her sparkling dark eyes.

"Only five years," said Janis. "And you went to college early."

"But you worked before law school," said Judy.

"That didn't make time stand still," said Janis.

They weren't arguing, Andrew realised. It was a friendship game. His belief that he could read the situation was returning. He liked these young women. He hoped that wasn't just the wine they'd been enjoying at lunch.

"So what do you two do for the Governor?" said Joe.

"Policy development," said Judy. The answer was out of her mouth before Joe could finish his question.

"Which is code for whatever he needs," said Janis.

"Hard job?" said Cynthia archly.

"Depends," said Janis evenly.

"This is our first day off in a month," said Judy.

"Would you like us to get you drunk?" said Rosemary.

"Not yet," said Janis.

"I don't drink," said Judy. "But maybe I should learn."

"Would you like to go swimming?" said Joe.

"It's been declared a topless beach," said Rosemary. A friendly warning.

"No swimming right after eating," said Sally.

Andrew poured wine for the two intruders. Judy started to reach for her glass but Shiva picked it up and moved it out of her reach. "Thank you, God" she said, which made Shiva laugh. She continued to list slightly in the Indian's direction.

"Judy was up all last night," said Janis. "She'll probably pass out even if she doesn't have any wine."

"Janis says I *submerge* myself in work," said Judy, leaning further towards Shiva. "'A bad habit,' she says."

"Her only bad habit," said Janis.

"And now you plan to submerge yourself in Shiva?" said Rosemary.

"Oh, excuse me," said Judy, sitting upright again. "It's just, I finished these briefing papers for the Governor – about zoning changes…constitutional issues…land tax – and then I had an hour to go home and put some things in a suitcase – he only invited us this morning – and the plane ride was too short to go to sleep, and then we went to his famous house, and I thought a nap would be nice, but before we finished unpacking we had to leave, and now I don't know whose house I'm in and I want to put my head down and your husband looks soft. Sorry."

"I think that sums it up nicely," said Rosemary. "Go into the living room, Shiva dear, and sit on the couch and put a pillow on your lap and let the poor child close her eyes for half an hour. She's about to throw up from sleepiness, and that wouldn't be fair to her or Cathy's rugs."

The two of them went into the living room as instructed. Andrew looked across the table into the next room and saw that Judy had already curled up on the sofa. Shiva was gently stroking her head, brushing the hair out of her face.

"Are you two friends," said Sally, "or just co-workers?"

"Friends," said Janis. "Have to be. We share an office that's the size of a small bathroom. She's hopeless and brilliant. The Justice she clerked for says God wants her to be a professor, but she has to get some real world experience first."

"'Real world' as in Massachusetts politics?" said Andrew. "Isn't that kind of the deep end of the pool?"

"I'm teaching her to tread water," said Janis, looking back at Andrew. *We both know all about treading water, don't we?* she seemed to be saying. How could she know that?

"I think school's out," said Rosemary, looking into the living room. "Has she passed the bar yet?"

"Oh, yes," said Janis. "In D.C. and in several states. It took me two tries just in New York." Janis looked around the room. "So God belongs to you," she said to Rosemary. "Who do the other men belong to?"

"He's mine," said Cynthia, pointing at Joe without much enthusiasm.

"I'm Cathy," said Sally. "Andrew and I are your hosts."

"Thanks," said Janis, briefly appraising her. "This is quite an imposition. Working for the Governor, we get used to radical changes of plan, but you didn't sign up for this. Do you even have enough beds?"

"We do," said Sally, appraising her back. Were they competitors or confederates? Andrew often couldn't figure women out, to be honest.

"Just not enough men," said Janis.

Rosemary laughed. "So why did you leave your job at a New York law firm to share an office the size of a loo?"

"Politics is more interesting than bond indentures. I think the Governor may wind up in the White House. I want to be one of those people on *West Wing*."

"Have you slept with him yet?" said Cynthia.

It was a stupendously rude question, considering the circumstances – a younger, *un*famous woman interrogated by a recognisable journalist in unfamiliar surroundings – but Janis batted it back easily. "He doesn't do that anymore," she said. And what was more impressive: the question went away.

If Rosemary was unembarrassed Venus, Janis was Athena disguised as an American. That wouldn't work, though. Athena was a virgin. Andrew doubted Janis was. Did he hope she was or hope she wasn't? He continued to like the idea that she would undress without embarrassment.

The conversation around the table continued for a while. Sally offered ice cream and strawberries. Joe got up to help her. Rosemary asked Shiva if he wanted some but he signalled from the sofa that he did not. Joe disappeared. Janis said she might go swimming if someone would come with her. No one offered. Part of Andrew wanted to but he couldn't figure out how. The party was losing focus.

"Shiva and I will go get more lobsters," said Rosemary, "or steak if it has to be that. Those who need naps will take naps."

Rosemary looked at Andrew and said nothing, meaning that he should go upstairs and do just that.

He didn't argue, but he didn't move.

"What about me?" said Cynthia.

"You could go upstairs and fuck your husband," said Rosemary blandly. She probably meant it as a joke.

"I've done my bit for today," said Cynthia. It was a decent come-back, but she looked offended. The rest of the guests politely pretended not to have heard the interchange. There seemed to be a backstory Andrew didn't know.

Rosemary asked Janis if she could get Judy upstairs so Shiva could come with her to the lobster monger. Janis said she could if Shiva would help her.

"Is 'lobster monger' a word?" said Cynthia. She was trying to rejoin the group, Andrew decided.

"It's two words," said Rosemary.

Before anyone could do anything, however, there was another phone call. The ringing was coming from the living room. Andrew got up quickly and felt briefly dizzy. Shouldn't have had wine at lunch. For some reason it was important that he stop the ringing. Mustn't let it alarm Judy. They had to get her upstairs without fully waking her. She was important to their plans in some as-yet-undisclosed way. He went towards the sound but there wasn't a source. Judy was stirring like a sleeper having a bad dream. It wasn't the sound the landline made. Shiva reached between the sofa cushions and extracted a mobile phone. He handed it to Andrew. Andrew recognised the phone as Cathy's. She'd insisted on having a red one – so she wouldn't lose it, she said. Like she was the commander of a nuclear missile site, Andrew had once told her, and the President had to be able to get her within five rings. It was a movie from the '50s they'd seen on television once.

The ringing stopped. It wasn't the President. The message on the screen said it was Eleanor. Andrew handed the phone to Rosemary.

Joe reappeared. "I'll help you," he said to Shiva, who still had Judy's head in his lap. He picked Judy up in his arms and carried her upstairs without difficulty. "Can you bring her bag?"

"I'll bring it," said Rosemary.

Andrew realised that would give her a brief opportunity to get Joe's views regarding his long walk with Shiva. What a clever woman she was. One had to acknowledge that Lady Rosemary was not a *nice* woman, but she was certainly skillful, both in and out of bed.

7

Andrew woke up with a start, lying on a bed that was supposed to have Cathy in it. Or some woman, at least. He was alone. It felt like late afternoon. He lay still to let reality crystallise. He got some of his best ideas that way.

He'd fallen asleep with his running shoes on. Rosemary had refused to let him dry dishes and insisted he go upstairs. It was as if his mind had been unable to cope and had simply shut down. His mind now seemed to be engaged again, which was reassuring.

Cathy hadn't gone to Germany. The evidence for this was that Eleanor was calling her. And she hadn't called the landline because she still wasn't talking to her father.

Andrew hadn't answered Cathy's phone when Eleanor called because he didn't know what to say to her. If Cathy hadn't gone to Germany, where was she? And why had she run away? Perhaps he didn't want to answer those questions.

Andrew hadn't told Sally that Eleanor had called because he thought he maybe had a better chance of finding out what Sally was up to if she didn't know he knew she'd lied to him about Cathy. Rosemary was certain Sally was "up to" something.

If he did confront Sally, she would presumably say Cathy had told her to tell him she'd gone to Germany, quote, so as not to worry you any more than necessary with important guests coming unquote. But was he supposed to not care about his daughter? It was getting complicated.

The important guests were all over the place. As Andrew was going upstairs, Sally had announced she was taking Rosemary and Joe to the whaling museum. She had called and learned it was going to close at five, and Joe wanted to see it. They could go to the store afterwards and buy steak. Its business was so heavily weekend oriented that it stayed open late on Saturdays. Cynthia had said she didn't approve of whaling and would Shiva please take her for a walk? Andrew assumed the Governor's overworked staff members were taking their own naps. He would have checked on them, or at least on Janis since Judy was presumably sound asleep, but that was something only the hostess could do.

There was nothing to be done about his office being moved – or what that portended – except pray that Joe and Shiva decided they liked each other. So far the signs were good, though Andrew wished Cynthia would stop flirting with Shiva, despite Rosemary's insistence that it would turn out to be helpful. If Joe decided to care, the deal could collapse in a heartbeat.

Andrew's own heart rate jumped at that thought, and then he felt tired again. They say if you are only in the shallow first stages of sleep, when you wake up you don't think you've been asleep. So maybe he'd gone back to sleep and what came next was a dream. It felt like a memory though.

He and Sally were in bed the first night, doing intimacy without sex, at which she was quite proficient. This was several hours before he'd gone downstairs and found Rosemary in the pantry. Rosemary naked sort of blotted out everything else, but being in bed with Sally was coming back. They'd been lying next to each other, not touching. She'd said she didn't plan to touch him but it was impossible not to wonder if she'd meant it. Cathy hadn't initiated in six weeks. He pretended he didn't know how long it had been, but he did.

After a bit Sally spoke, very softly, which was like being touched unexpectedly. "Did she talk to you in the dark?"

"Cathy?"

"Yes."

"No," said Andrew.

"She talked to me," said Sally.

"Yes."

"I told you we'd shared a bottle of wine the night we finished getting the house ready."

"Yes."

"After dinner she said she wanted to see what I looked like in some of her clothes."

"That was after she'd told you everything?"

"Everything about you."

Andrew thought about that for a minute.

"We came up here," said Sally. "I undressed."

"As you did for me," said Andrew.

"Cathy pulled various dresses and blouses out of the closet and I put them on. 'You're good in that,' she'd say, or 'wrong colour.'"

"Her clothes fit you well," said Andrew.

"A bit tight in the bust," said Sally.

"Cynthia admired your breasts," said Andrew, remembering the conversation that morning on the porch.

"She was overexcited," said Sally. "She wanted to touch them. I could tell. I would have let her put sun cream on me but I wasn't sure she could handle it."

"I suppose you don't want me to touch them either?" said Andrew.

"Oh, I'd like it very much, but it wouldn't be consistent with the master plan."

"Which is?"

"That's up to you," said Sally. "I assume you have one, though in my experience most people don't. But isn't the idea here to keep the billionaires happy?"

"And their wives," said Andrew. "You don't much like Cynthia, do you?"

"Not an issue," said Sally. "I'm the hostess. I have to be nice. I just get impatient with women who lack self-awareness. But let me finish. Cathy and I went through maybe half a dozen outfits, some necklaces, some rings. 'Stay with me,' she said finally. Nothing more. So we both put on tee shirts and got under the doona. We turned out the lights and lay side by side, a foot apart, the way you and I are now. Just when I thought she must have gone to sleep, she spoke."

"Just as you did a few minutes ago," Andrew had said.

"And it startled me the way my speaking startled you," Sally had said. "She told me about kissing one of your house guests, last summer."

"A kiss that started out as a hug," said Andrew.

"Yes. She told you about it too?"

"Last May," said Andrew. "The story was part of a discussion that felt like an argument that led to our hiring you. I thought it had to do with the strain of entertaining every weekend, and the prospect of being alone during the week."

"She asked if she could kiss me," said Sally.

Andrew said nothing.

"I do that sort of thing," said Sally. Pause. "Not exclusively." Pause. "I'm flexible."

"How useful," said Andrew.

"That was all," said Sally. Clearly it wasn't. "Well, almost all. I woke once in the night and discovered that she'd reached towards me in her sleep. Her hand was touching mine."

"But earlier, had you kissed her?"

"Of course."

There was a sound in the hall. The memory vanished. Andrew got off the bed and opened the door. It was the Governor of Massachusetts. No Janis. "Ah, Andrew," he said. "For a minute I thought there was no one home." He seemed to regard going upstairs in someone else's house as normal behaviour.

"Aren't you supposed to be attending to Lydia, talking to her about her mother or something?" George seemed to be taking over the weekend.

"Well, I would be," said the Governor. "Come downstairs. I need a beer."

"Just let me check on a few things," said Andrew. He walked up and down the hall quietly opening bedroom doors. Judy was in Shiva and Rosemary's room, still asleep. There was no sign of the others.

"I would be comforting Lydia even as we speak," the Governor repeated as Andrew opened the refrigerator to find a beer. "I would be doing just that if one of those naughty girls I've dumped on you hadn't left clothes in the washing machine."

"Oh my," said Andrew.

"Which Lydia found. Which means I need a bed for the

night myself, because she's kicked me out."

"Sorry," said Janis, coming in with a copy of *Moby Dick* in her hand. Andrew decided he liked her freckles. "You made us leave in such a rush, I forgot. Apologies for eavesdropping." She said this to Andrew. "I was on the porch around the corner."

"Why were you doing laundry at all?" said the Governor, more curious than annoyed, it seemed to Andrew. He doubted George even knew how to run a washing machine.

"You made us leave Boston in a rush too, if you recall, Governor. You called at eight in the morning. I normally do my laundry on the weekends. So I had to pack some dirty clothes."

"Black lace underpants and bra?" said George.

"Do you want a beer, Janis?" said Andrew. He liked imagining her in black lace.

"No alcohol before six," she said.

"And no sex after alcohol?" said Andrew, and immediately felt foolish. He wasn't sure why he'd said that. George and Janis ignored him. "You need another one, George?"

"I'm good."

Cathy's phone rang again. Andrew pulled it out of his pocket and looked at the screen but didn't answer it. "I suppose I should tell you what's going on," he said to both of them. "Come sit on the porch."

"So that woman who introduced herself as Cathy isn't your wife, but you're pretending she is?" said Janis when he had finished outlining the situation. She spoke as if it were an interesting public policy question that would benefit from sound analysis. She seemed to enjoy analysis. Or maybe it was "situations" she enjoyed – and being unfazed by *anything*. Working for the Governor would have given her plenty of situations to practise on.

"Of course, George will realise Sally isn't Cathy as soon as she gets back from the whaling museum," said Andrew.

"I've known Cathy since she was a little girl," the Governor explained. "Our parents knew each other. I flattered myself that she had a crush on me when she was fourteen."

"Every girl in Boston has had a crush on you at some point, George," said Andrew.

"So you want us to pretend Sally's Cathy too?" said Janis, ignoring the matter of crushes.

"That would be helpful," said Andrew.

"Who is she?" said the Governor, standing up. He signalled that another beer would be acceptable after all, and the three of them went back into the kitchen.

"Well, I don't really know," said Andrew. "Cathy hired her as a general helper and companion. Florence and Eleanor are both away this summer. Cathy thought she'd be lonely."

"Does she look like Cathy?" the Governor asked.

"Little bit. They can wear each other's clothes. *This* Cathy is younger, with darker hair." He paused. "Bit bustier."

"And you're sleeping with her?" said Janis.

"Sleeping in the same bed," said Andrew, "but…"

"Too much information," said the Governor.

"So will this Cathy know that the Governor knows the real Cathy," said Janis, "and therefore know she's a fraud?"

"She will if she thinks about it for more than a second," said Andrew. "I've told them all that George and I are old friends."

"And that at least is true," said the Governor.

"So what will this Cathy do?" said Janis.

"We're about to find out," said Andrew.

Sally came in the door, followed by Rosemary and Joe. As soon as she saw the Governor, whose face every sentient

American adult would recognise, she came straight over and gave him a hug and a kiss on the cheek. George seized the opportunity to pat her on the ass, which made Andrew smile. They'd never met, but they were going to pretend they didn't know that.

"Whaling was ridiculous," said Rosemary to anyone who would listen.

"Dangerous," said Joe. "But *immensely* profitable." He was carrying plastic bags full of steaks and other groceries, which he put on the kitchen counter. "I think we have enough," he said.

"I think you overdid it," said Sally, smiling at the big man.

"You'll find I tend to do that," he said, smiling back.

"I look forward to it," said Sally.

It felt like they were speaking some sort of code. Rosemary gave Andrew a cautionary look. He didn't know what it meant but he kept silent. "Where's Shiva?" she said.

"I thought he and Cynthia went for a walk," said Andrew. "But I've been napping…as instructed."

"He and Cynthia definitely went for a walk," said Janis. "She was quite insistent. Wanted to show him whatever she and Sally had seen on their run, she said."

"There wasn't anything to see but sand and sea grass," said Sally.

And Cynthia's breasts, Andrew said to himself. She was selectively prudish, evidently.

"They didn't invite you?" said Rosemary.

"I didn't want to go," said Janis. "To be honest, sitting still for an hour suddenly sounded very appealing. And I've been improving myself by reading Melville." She held up her copy of *Moby Dick* as if to prove it.

Well brought up, Andrew said to himself. Reads the book

her pretentious host puts in all the guest rooms to prove he's educated.

The freckles definitely worked. They allowed her to look old-fashioned and modern at the same time. Or was it wise and innocent? Anyway, it was a winning combination.

Andrew realised he'd been looking at Janis too long. "George will be staying with us too," he said, addressing Sally.

"It's complicated," said the Governor, as if in explanation.

"Sleeping arrangements?" said Rosemary quietly.

"We'll have to see," said Sally. And then in a louder voice, "Sweetheart, we ought to get the water boiling for the lobsters. Maybe Joe can help you."

"Whatever you ask," said Joe, smiling at Sally.

There was a low stone and concrete construction behind the house, with a long iron grill on which it would be possible to cook several dozen steaks at once. There was an oversized pot resting upside down at one end. Andrew explained that it was easier and safer to fill the pot with water before they started the fire. "I should probably have a long hose," he said, "but I don't, so we have to use these jerry cans." He and Joe began filling the cans from the faucet on the side of the house and pouring the contents into the pot. After a couple of round trips, Joe wanted to check the pot for stability. Then he wanted to be sure that, with the pot already on the grill, air would get to the fire. "I understand fire, being an engineer," he explained, "and I used to build fires when I was a kid, of course, but these days I don't get much chance to barbeque." He paused. "Cyn thinks that's un-American."

"Coming from Texas."

"I suppose that's the explanation," said Joe. "She doesn't know shit about barbeques, of course. Her Texas is air-conditioned. Doesn't like getting her hands dirty. But she thinks I should have one in Greenwich."

"I don't suppose Shiva and Rosemary know much about barbeques either," said Andrew, spotting an opening.

Joe was now lying prone on the ground, looking through the holes in the back wall of the construction that would allow air to be drawn in by the fire, once it got going. "Rosemary's crazy," he said matter-of-factly. "Smart, but crazy. What she knows about I could not predict. But Shiva's tougher than you'd expect. He's not afraid of getting his hands dirty. He's just tired of having to do so. I see how this thing works now. But you have to pull out the charcoal from the last fire." He came around to the front of the grill and began scraping out the remains of the previous weekend's barbeque. "You should have done this earlier. When it rains, the charcoal gets soaked and then it's messier to deal with. Have you got some old newspapers I can dump it on?" By this point his hands and arms were black and his shirt front was streaked with mud and charcoal.

Andrew went around to the back door that went directly into the pantry and brought back a pile of last weekend's Sunday papers. "I should be doing this," he said to Joe.

"No sweat," said his guest. "I *like* getting my hands dirty – in case you haven't figured that out yet."

"So you and Shiva could get along?" said Andrew. He held his breath as Joe considered his answer.

"As men, yes. He has guts. He has brains. I admire what he's done with the unholy jumble of businesses he got handed when his father died. I just worry about his energy level. I worry about our not being able to make decisions because he's too tired. Or worn out from being sweet and reasonable with his impossible brothers."

95

"The walk to the lighthouse?" said Andrew.

"Oh, that. Yeah, he doesn't take any exercise at all, as far as I can figure out. I'm talking about *mental* energy. But we'll see. We haven't talked about strategy yet – what we actually do with this business you want us to jointly own. If we could agree on a general course of action and he could give me authority over tactical moves that might help."

Andrew's heart sank, but he decided he should wait until he could talk to Rosemary.

"There, I think it's cleaned out. Now let's finish filling the lobster pot and get a fire started."

"You want to go in and wash your hands?"

"No, under the tap is fine."

Three more round trips with the jerry cans and Joe had another question: "You didn't know about cleaning out the charcoal, did you Andrew?"

"Cathy usually does it."

"Shitty job for a girl," said Joe. "Cyn would never consider cleaning out wet charcoal with her bare hands." He laughed at the idea.

"Cathy doesn't seem to mind," said Andrew. "New Englanders are like that. Hard winters and all."

"But she forgot this week?"

Andrew began to feel apprehensive. "Guess so."

"What are we using for tinder and where are the logs, and most important, where are the matches?"

"I normally use the previous weekend's newspapers," said Andrew.

"But I've kind of messed them up," said Joe. "Where are the logs? I hope you keep them dry."

He did not. There was a year-old cord of wood neatly

stacked further away from the house, but it wasn't, in fact, under cover. Andrew had brought the matches, however, which was a relief. He was beginning to feel totally incompetent.

Joe fetched two logs and stood them on their ends beside the grill. He took a folding knife out of his pocket. "I'm going to teach you some woodcraft, Andrew. I used to be a boy scout." He drove the knife repeatedly into one of the logs and began to peel off bits of bark and then dry splinters. "I don't suppose you know what 'squaw wood' is, Andrew?"

"No."

"It's dead branches that haven't fallen all the way to the ground, so they're dry. You go wander around your yard and see if you can collect some. Start with that tree over there."

Andrew obeyed – wandering around felt like all he was good for – and within a few minutes brought back an armful.

"I probably didn't need to make all this splinter tinder, with the squaw wood you've got on the property," said Joe, "but it's a good thing for you to know about."

"You mean in case there's a nuclear winter and we all have to depend on our survival skills? That's why I live in Manhattan – so there's no danger of surviving."

Joe laughed. "You never know when survival skills will come in handy." He began to build a little tepee of splinters and then squaw wood twigs and then larger branches. He slid two of the logs under the grill on either side of this combustible construction, and then laid medium-size branches across the logs. "Now you repeat that further along," he said. "I think we'll need three modules – one under the lobster pot and two for the steaks. Here, you don't know shit about building a fire, do you?"

"I'm afraid I'm pretty urban," said Andrew, who had never been a boy scout. He was trying his best to get honourably dirty but his body resisted lying prone the way Joe had, so he was sitting cross-legged.

Joe laughed. "That's right. Remember, you'll want to add another log to each module once the fire gets going. But you don't want to do it too soon. And you want to take the wet bark off the logs if you can because that will be the moment of maximum vulnerability for the fire."

"I never thought of a fire as being vulnerable," said Andrew. A girl with freckles was another story.

Joe pondered Andrew's statement for a minute. "So Cathy's always made the fire?"

"Usually."

"Why not today?"

Andrew was working on an answer, but Joe cut him off. "Listen, Andrew, I don't want to play games. This person who's just taken Rosemary and me to the whaling museum isn't your wife. She'd never been there before. But I knew it already because I do *very thorough* research. I Googled you. I had someone go through *all* the pages. I've seen your wedding pictures in the Boston newspapers of twenty years ago. *This* Cathy is a pretty good imitation, but she's not the girl you married."

Andrew let out his breath. "Do you want the long version or the short version?"

"We gotta keep the fire company for a while," said Joe.

"Well, to start with, you're right of course. But it wasn't something I planned. I don't even know who this Cathy is, to be honest."

"Funny thing is," said Joe, "I feel like I've met her before. But give me the long version."

It took about half an hour. They got the fire well established.

Joe was a patient listener. "So you and your real missus have been hanging on by your fingernails, it sounds like," he said when Andrew was finished.

"I suppose we have," said Andrew. "One tries not to focus on those things."

"I may need to suggest another approach, if we decide to work together."

"A new model every other year?" said Andrew.

"I wasn't talking about that," said Joe. "What I meant was, I believe in acknowledging reality. It's healthier." He paused. "And as you might imagine, I don't like people keeping anything a secret from me – not that they normally can."

Andrew felt dizzy. "There's something else I ought to tell you then," he said after a moment. Now he felt like he was throwing himself off a cliff. Or maybe he'd been in free fall all weekend.

"Shoot," said Joe.

"I'm having a little trouble at my firm. They may be trying to get me to retire."

Joe thought about that for a minute. "Aren't you kinda young for that?" he said.

"'Retire' is a euphemism," said Andrew.

"Getting pushed out?" said Joe.

"That's what it looks like."

"Those phone calls?"

"Guy who's technically my boss being unpleasant."

"Technically?"

"You're right, Joe. If I'm facing reality, he is my boss and he can fire me." Andrew felt better, oddly, just saying that. Joe didn't say anything so he went on. "Investment banking firms are organised to permit self-delusion. We all call ourselves 'managing directors,' even though we don't manage anything. Bonuses are mostly secret. The only way you really know where you stand is by seeing where your office is. And I'm getting moved to a smaller one this weekend."

"Any particular reason your boss wants to jettison you?"

"He's new in the job. I haven't produced much in the past two years. I come up with my own ideas. I try to concentrate on significant transactions. Success is unpredictable. Pushing me out is a way for him to establish his authority."

"Stupid way to run a business," said Joe. "Does your technical boss happen to dislike you for some reason?"

"Oh, probably. He didn't go to Harvard. One tries not to focus on those things."

Joe laughed. "That again."

"Wall Street is a tightrope," said Andrew. "Not a good idea to look down."

Joe was silent for a couple of minutes. "I wish I could tell you this deal is going to happen. But I can't. Or not yet." He was silent for another minute. "Let's pretend we haven't had this conversation," he said finally.

"Sure," said Andrew. He had no idea what he was agreeing to.

"I don't want you looking down," said Joe, evidently reading his mind. "But going back to our earlier discussion," said Joe, "what I wanted to ask was, have you got any particular attachment to this substitute Cathy? Because I find her quite amusing."

"Be my guest," said Andrew.

"I'm your guest already," said Joe, standing up. "But I want to be a good one. Is it safe to leave the fire while we get cleaned up?"

"Always has been in the past," said Andrew. "But you go in. I'll watch it for a while."

I'm not totally stupid, Andrew told himself, just terrified. Maybe if he sat quietly, useful ideas would present themselves. They didn't. He reverted to his fall-back strategy for coping with anxiety: thinking about sex.

When the men had finished their port and Andrew had gone up to his freezing room on that comic opera shooting party weekend he'd been sent to as an associate, Venetia of the bathtub was already warming his bed. "Get in quickly before I die," she'd said in a hoarse whisper.

She was wearing flannel pyjamas. She laughed at his nightshirt. She made him put his arms around her and warm her up. For two or three minutes neither of them spoke. Parts of him began to express curiosity about their plans.

"We're going to kiss a lot," she said, as if in answer. "But that's all we'll do."

"I thought you wanted to 'bag' me," said Andrew. There'd been a lot of wine at dinner and he was feeling bold.

"For the purposes of this weekend, I already have." She kissed him on the mouth. He responded. "And you're married," she continued.

"I am," he said.

"With an infant daughter."

"Eleanor."

"And you've never been unfaithful."

"Correct."

"So you need to be punished."

"For what? I haven't been unfaithful yet. All I've done is think about it. I thought about it all through dinner, by the way. How could I not?"

"Exactly," said Venetia.

"You're a terrible tease, you know?"

"I know."

"We came down to dinner separately. You never spoke to me during cocktails. You were seated far away down the table. You never looked at me."

"That's how the game is played," said Venetia.

"All I could think about was you stepping into the bathtub and introducing yourself. That and the prospect of keeping each other warm tonight."

"Punishments are for things that aren't a person's fault, things they had no choice about."

"Is that so?"

"You don't know anything about punishment, do you? It's the main thing you learn at an English boarding school."

Andrew didn't reply.

"You have to be punished for thinking about me precisely *because* you can't help it. I plan to *enjoy* the fact that you can't stop thinking about me. And I am not going to let you be unfaithful," she continued, "until you are desperate to be so." She kissed him again. "It's deeply philosophical – or maybe I mean theological. Transgression and retribution as one. Wanting me will be painful because you are a healthy young man. Having me will be painful because you will feel guilty about it. It's like taking a barge through a lock. You have to get the water to the level of the next stage before you can proceed."

"This is a weird conversation," said Andrew. His American soul could recognise witchcraft, even light-hearted witchcraft.

"I will give you my address," she said, ignoring his outburst. "I live alone, in a tiny house in Chelsea. Very fashionable neighbourhood. This coming Wednesday – that's Tuesday night if you haven't been to bed – you will stand on the doorstep without ringing the bell. At precisely two in morning I will open the door. We'll see what level the water is at then. But first we have to practise being in love. So kiss me some more, but make your hands behave."

Rosemary materialised in front of him. He was startled. He was embarrassed to have been thinking about Venetia. He half expected Rosemary to chide him for doing so. He didn't think he'd tell Rosemary about Venetia. Or Janis. *Tell* Janis, that is. Not that the subject of Venetia needed to come up. "Joe's figured out about Sally-Cathy," he said without standing up.

"I was going to tell you that. She had trouble finding the museum. And Joe misses nothing."

"He thinks you're crazy."

"I'm doing the best I can," said Rosemary.

"I don't think you're crazy," said Andrew. It sounded like a profession of love.

"Of course you don't," said Rosemary. "It's Joe I had to confuse. I had to make sure he didn't start hitting on me, which could have troubled Shiva."

"Not an issue," said Andrew. "He's decided he likes my wife – Sally-Cathy that is."

"Which leaves us the minor problem of Cynthia," said Rosemary. "I'm afraid she's turning out to be surplus to requirements."

"I thought she and Shiva went for a walk," said Andrew.

"That was so she could take her top off again, I expect. He'll have liked that, but it won't get her anywhere."

"Really?"

"Cynthia has too many angles," said Rosemary. "I have too many angles. Shiva wants soft."

"I like your angles," said Andrew.

"Stand up," said Rosemary. He complied. "You need to go clean up, play host, pay attention, not drink too much. I put fresh clothes in the servant's room for you. And think about this. Nothing we can do will save Cynthia's marriage, and it shouldn't be saved. She'll be cashing in her pre-nup, as those contracts are evidently called, by the end of the summer. Not a bad pay-check for what? – two hundred fucks. The only issue with Cynthia is to keep her from getting in the way of the romance we care about."

"Joe and Shiva – metaphorically, that is."

"I told you you had potential."

"You did?"

"Well, maybe I forgot to say it, but I thought it." She kissed him – briefly but on the lips. "You're a very smart man. You look shattered, by the way, but I can't fix that right now. We'll deal with that tonight. Go take a shower. I'll wander in the garden for a while."

8

When Andrew came out of the servant's room after taking a shower and putting on the clean clothes Rosemary had laid out for him, the only person in evidence was Janis. She was sitting on a sofa in the living room, looking composed, still reading *Moby Dick*. It occurred to him that Janis was a lawyer. Rosemary had wanted a lawyer. It was possible they had a plan, even if he didn't know what it was. Plans need to marinate sometimes, so he put the thought away, but he liked it that his brain was functioning.

He also liked it that shipwrecked Janis might have a role. Perhaps she was noble young Ferdinand and Andrew himself was Miranda. A little cross-dressing never bothered Shakespeare. Joe was turning into a very intelligent version of Caliban. What made him a monster was single-mindedness. Rosemary was Prospero, of course. Why "of course?" Why not Shiva, who so wanted the role? Not strong enough. Making magic required force of character, which Rosemary certainly had, whereas Shiva – Rosemary's phrase – "liked soft."

Invention always cheered Andrew up, even when his ideas were silly. He felt clever again, and therefore resilient. He had survived twenty years on Wall Street. He reckoned he could be assumed to have inner resources.

"Have you never read it before?" he said to Janis from across the room. "And would you like a drink yet?" Rosemary had told him to play host, and she was right in recognising that it would calm him. He'd done this perhaps a hundred times, had people for the weekend he needed to charm. The routine was reassuring.

"'No' to both questions," said Janis brightly, looking up. "How about you? And have you heard from your wife?" she added quickly.

Andrew came over and sat down facing her. He hadn't intended it, but the chair he had chosen gave him a view of the stairs, the doors onto the porch and through the archway into the dining room. If this were a murder mystery, he said to himself, I'd be perfectly positioned to collect evidence. And maybe it is, he added cheerfully.

Janis had somehow managed to find a shower. Her short red hair was still a bit damp. She was perfectly dressed for a Nantucket Saturday night, in leather sandals and a skirt and blouse, which she had somehow managed to iron. "Organised" was the word that came to mind. But "polite" was in there too. For Janis, Andrew suspected, nothing was ever someone else's fault. She would always turn out to have the right clothes, find an iron without making a fuss, laugh at other people's stories, never be late for dinner, and go to bed before the hostess started to yawn.

"No, Cathy hasn't called. I'm sure she's fine," he said. "But as to *Moby Dick*, I read it thirty years ago. Strange book. If you do manage to finish it, you'll be the first house guest we've ever had who has."

"Strange, yes," said Janis. "So far the narrator has spent a night in bed with a tattooed harpooner. But it's too long to finish in a weekend, even if it rained and you did nothing but read."

"You can take your copy home if you want," said Andrew. "We have extras. And I am very glad it isn't raining."

"Too many people?" said Janis. "Too many sub-plots?"

"No, look, I'm delighted you're here. I'm delighted George is here. I've known him forever, you know. We have plenty of room. I prefer a bigger group, actually. But speaking of room, have you and Judy been assigned beds yet? I haven't been a very good host, I'm afraid."

"Not to worry," said Janis. "Cathy is an *excellent* hostess." If Andrew needed Sally to be Cathy, Janis would cooperate. "I'm in the bunk room," she added. "I seem to have it to myself. I've been given towels."

"George has the big back bedroom, I assume?"

"As befits the Governor of the Commonwealth," said Janis. She made a bit of a joke of it, but he realised she had regard for the office. "I'll admit that I peeked in. Fabulous four-poster bed."

"And Judy...?"

"Well, actually, I don't know where she is," said Janis. "Last time I saw her, Joe was carrying her upstairs and Rosemary was following with her suitcase."

"What's she like?" said Andrew. "Sorry. Bit of a *non sequitur*. Whole weekend feels like that." He wished he could tell her everything – about his marriage, about the politics in his office – but that wouldn't have been appropriate. Or smart. Or likely to impress a girl, for that matter.

"You met Judy at lunch, remember?" said Janis.

"Only briefly. She fell asleep pretty soon after she arrived."

"I suppose she did," said Janis. "She works too hard. I sometimes think she's trying to impress the Governor, but that's silly. She's already impressed him or she wouldn't have the job. Her CV impressed him. The recommendation of a Supreme Court Justice had to impress him."

"How did you impress him?"

"I interview well."

Andrew thought about that for a moment but Janis didn't elaborate. "You're good," he said finally.

"I am," she said without apology. "My mother said I'd make a fine mistress."

Was Janis warning him off or encouraging him to make an advance? The conversation was an awkward mixture of disclosure and reticence. It felt like a first date where you couldn't decide if the girl really liked you or was just being nice. With someone as nice as Janis, that would be particularly hard to tell.

Andrew elected to go back to the question of Judy. "The last time I saw your colleague, she was still asleep – on Shiva and Rosemary's bed." He paused. "You don't suppose she's still there, do you?"

"I keep reminding myself that I'm not her governess but I feel like I'm supposed to look out for her," said Janis.

Judy came in through the door to the porch just as Janis completed this confession, which made Andrew laugh.

Janis laughed too. "This *is* starting to feel like one of those drawing-room comedies, with all the entrances and exits perfectly timed."

"Oh, good," said Judy. "I was hoping I'd find you." She came over and sat down. "This is not a straight-forward situation,

Janis," she said without preliminary.

"Would you like privacy?" said Andrew.

"What for?" said Judy.

"It sounds like you wanted to talk to your friend."

"Well, I do," said Judy. "But I should be speaking to you as well, Andrew. It's your house, after all, so I assume you make the rules." She looked at Janis. "I'm supposed to call him 'Andrew', right?"

"Please do," said Andrew. "But there are no rules."

"Of course there are rules," said Judy. "They just aren't always transparent. That's why there are lawyers. Lawyers give advice. Or technically, they sell advice. Anyway, I need some. You can bill me later." She was no longer the sleepy girl who had arrived six hours earlier.

"I'm your host," said Andrew. "It's on the house."

"Go on," said Janis gently. Her affection for her small, intense colleague was manifest. It spoke well of her, Andrew thought.

"Apparently, I'm supposed to sleep with God."

"Shiva," said Andrew. Janis didn't react.

"My clothes are all hung up in his closet," said Judy. "My underwear is in the dresser in his room. My toothbrush is in his bathroom."

"You're not *required* to sleep with him," said Janis. "But who would have unpacked your bag?"

"No idea. At least there were only clean clothes to unpack," she said, giving Janis a sympathetic look.

"Well, pack them up again and come to the bunk room if you want to," said Janis. "Just because he's rich and famous, doesn't mean you have to share his bed."

She looked at Andrew. "Correct," he said.

"Oh, but I want to," said Judy. "Share his bed, that is. I love that phrase. I makes me feel like I'm in a cheap novel."

"You're a grown-up," said Janis.

"Well, no, I'm not. We both know that, but my mother's been dead for a while and it's time I grew up, and he seems very nice."

"And...?" said Janis.

"Well, the thing is, God's wife seems to approve. That's what I meant about the situation not being straight-forward. Or maybe I mean unconventional. I've just spent half an hour out in the garden talking to...what's her name again?"

"Rosemary," said Andrew. He'd forgotten about her being Prospero and arranging things. She was looking after Shiva's sex life so she'd be free to look after Andrew.

"Bit strange," said Judy, "but nice. And gorgeous. Just looking at her could make a person want to be a lesbian – which I'm not, by the way. That's not why I want to sleep with God. I *know* I like boys. I just haven't ever had one. Or one's never had me, if that's how it works. Anyway, gorgeous Rosemary said if Shiva – I suppose I should stop calling him God – if Shiva and I wanted to quote get to know each other better unquote – that's how she put it – she'd have no objection. I guess she's prepared to sleep in the bunkroom with you, Janis. She said Shiva's had a vasectomy so there's nothing to worry about. He has children by a previous wife, she said, and his family was already too complicated without his having any with her. I'm not sure she's happy about that – not having children, I mean – but she was completely open about it. I guess that's what being extremely rich does to you: you're allowed to talk about anything. Everyone else is essentially a servant. She said Shiva's really tired – not just from jet lag but from everything he has

110

to cope with in business – and she says he obviously finds me restful. I don't have any elbows, she said. I think that was it. She could tell by watching him when I went to sleep with my head in his lap. That was embarrassing, doing that, wasn't it?"

"Not really," said Andrew.

"So it looks like I'm about to have an adventure. Rosemary said if Shiva and I got along he'd probably take me to India. He has his own plane. Did you know he's a prince? She said I'd probably get to see a tiger in his forest. I said I expected I'd be frightened. She said being frightened is not a good strategy. 'All right, I won't be', I said." She finally paused. "So what do you think? Will the Governor give me time off?"

Andrew watched Janis consider several answers and reject them, all the while smiling at her friend. "The short answer is 'yes'," she said finally.

"Will you speak to him for me?"

"The Governor?"

"Definitely the Governor. I don't think you should speak to Shiva about this," said Judy. "He might be embarrassed, though maybe princes don't do embarrassed. Do you think he needs to speak to anyone to get time off? Rosemary said he badly needs time off, so maybe he doesn't know who to ask. Maybe I should help set the table." She stood up suddenly and went into the kitchen where Sally, who'd come downstairs as Judy was talking, was rattling glasses.

"That was simple," said Andrew.

"She's ready for an adventure," said Janis. "I just hope she doesn't get hurt too badly."

"Can't we hope she won't get hurt at all?" said Andrew.

"That's not how life works," said Janis.

"You're in love with the Governor, aren't you?" said

Andrew. It wasn't a question, really. It wasn't polite, either. He realised that as soon as he said it. Why was it a question he thought he needed to ask?

"I suppose it's obvious," said Janis, making no attempt to be offended.

"No," said Andrew. "It isn't. Your mother was right. You're very discreet. But just for a moment, sadness was there in your voice – sadness being love's companion. Sorry."

"You say lovely things," said Janis, leaning forward and touching his arm briefly. "But could we not talk about it?"

"Absolutely," said Andrew. What other lovely things had he said? "Does Judy know Sally isn't Cathy?" he added quickly, needing to change the subject.

"No, but I think I should tell her," said Janis. "As you've just seen, she blurts things out when they occur to her, and she's very observant, so there can be a lot of blurting. I'll tell her there's this mystery, and we're not talking about it. She should be fine." Janis paused. "But are *you* fine?"

"Could we not talk about it?" said Andrew. There wasn't anything to say, actually.

"Absolutely," said Janis. "And for the record, I'm not his mistress."

"I didn't mean to imply that you were," said Andrew. Subject closed.

It seemed to Andrew that she might have wanted to say something more, but they could both see the Governor coming down the stairs, which made that impossible. He was talking to someone over his shoulder as he did so. Then Shiva came into view. He'd said they'd met some years ago. They seemed to be getting along. "But you're on duty 24/7 too, I assume," the Indian was saying.

112

"Not like in the White House," said the Governor, coming over to Andrew and Janis. "I mean, theoretically I have more power than the President, at least within the Commonwealth. Criminal law is mostly a state matter, for example. If a judge condemns someone, I can pardon them. Which makes me God, same as you. Or God to the criminal in question." Both men laughed briefly as they sat down. Power agreed with them. "But if I leave Massachusetts – you know that Nantucket is part of Massachusetts, right? – if I leave, the Lieutenant Governor takes over. Of course, we don't have a military. I don't think the police count as such."

Shiva looked at Janis for confirmation. "There is no Massachusetts One," she said, which made all three men laugh. Janis was good at making men laugh.

"And there still isn't word from Cathy One?" said the Governor, leaning towards Andrew and whispering. "Shiva knows," he added.

"Joe told me," said Shiva. "He said that quote, if we're going to be partners, we have to share information. Interesting. I guess I've never had a partner."

Andrew liked the sound of that – Rosemary's not being Shiva's partner.

"I share information with Janis," said the Governor.

"But not everything," she said.

"If I told you everything, you'd have to lie. This way you can tell people you don't know the Governor's position on the bill – or whatever. I'm just protecting your reputation."

Janis smiled.

But you're happy to bring her to Nantucket, Andrew said to himself. And then aloud: "The answer to your question regarding Cathy is 'no.'"

"Is there a Shiva One?" said the Governor, politely shifting the discussion. "I mean, I assume you have a plane…"

"I do."

"…but do you have to be in touch with your business empire at all times?"

"I don't have to, probably, but I feel I should. There is always something going wrong. I feel an obligation to know about it, even if fixing it will take time."

"I have to know about everything," said the Governor, looking at Janis, "but that's because I'm an elected official and some reporter will ask me about it. A fire in Roxbury. A snow storm in North Adams. If someone is killed I have to issue a statement. If five people are killed, I have to go there and be on television. If I look like I don't care, I'll have to answer to the voters. But you don't have to answer to anyone, Shiva. Most of your empire isn't even public." George paused. "I suppose you have to answer to your family, though."

"I have to answer to my conscience," said the prince.

And tonight, you're going to deflower a virgin, Andrew said to himself. Which your wife has arranged. He looked at Janis. She looked back.

"Well, so do I," said the Governor. "You run for office, you choose a political career, you accept limitations, you have responsibilities. But that's interesting what you said Joe said about partners. I suppose it would be quite nice to be able to hand off some of the burden, to share information and to share duties."

"Sharing information I understand," said Shiva. "I tell Rosemary everything. Well, almost everything. I spare her some of the details." He paused. Through the door into the dining room, Judy had come into view with placemats and napkins.

"She claims to find business boring," Shiva continued. "It is an English affectation – not unlike my being a vegetarian most of the time. But the burden of responsibility cannot be shared. It can only be laid aside completely."

"That's what happens when I leave Massachusetts."

"You can put your cares aside like that?"

"For a few days, I can. And I promise you, the Lieutenant Governor loves it. He prays for a snow storm in North Adams so he can be on television and have name recognition, which will make all the difference when I move on and he wants to run for Governor."

"Are you planning to run for President?" said Shiva with a twinkle.

"The Governor hasn't decided," said Janis.

"The Governor needs a drink," said George. "There was a time when one could obtain a gin and tonic in this house." He started to stand up, but Janis put a hand on his arm.

"I'll get it," she said. As she herself stood up, Joe came down the stairs.

"Light on the gin," said the Governor.

"Meaning none?" she said.

"Oh, a little," he said. "It's a Saturday night," he explained to the other men. "Then again, it's Saturday night. Good weather. A few beers. We could have a drowning."

"Meaning you'd need to issue a statement?" said Shiva.

"Exactly."

"Anyone else want a drink?" said Janis.

"Well, I don't *need* to issue a statement," said Joe, "but I may." He gestured towards the stairs with his head. "Normal strength, please," he added. Andrew and Shiva both declined. Janis went into the kitchen.

115

"Nice girl," said the Governor once she had disappeared. "Extremely competent – and in love with me, I fear."

"You shouldn't have let her do that," said Shiva.

"George has this problem," said Andrew.

One does sometimes, Andrew reflected, have experiences with persons of the opposite sex that split one open as lightning can a tree. Rosemary had had that effect on Andrew. He hoped to survive. Venetia of the bathtub had left her mark. But this happened to George all the time. He was supposed to be a lady killer but, actually, what distinguished him was excess susceptibility.

Andrew knew this because they had discussed it in some detail shortly after two a.m. one winter night outside Quincy House. You have to be pretty drunk to stand around outdoors in Cambridge in January, so of course they achieved major insights about the nature of the universe and whether a girl named Andrea was a goddess or a manipulative bitch. George took the former view. He always did, until he got tired of the girl. Andrew never went out with girls like Andrea – never had the courage to pursue them – so he tended to be dismissive of them.

"Love complicates relationships," Shiva was saying.

"Is that why you people do arranged marriages?" said Joe.

"No. But it gets things off on the right foot."

"Not being in love?" said Joe.

"No expectations. Not knowing each other before the wedding. After that, of course, there are no guarantees. Sometimes one falls in love. It's not a matter of volition. That's why it's called 'falling.'"

Watching Shiva watch Judy appear and disappear as she set the table, Andrew decided he couldn't tell whether Shiva thought falling in love with someone was a blessing or a burden. He had no idea, really, what Rosemary and Shiva's marriage was like, beyond the reported shortage of "soft." He just wanted it to evaporate. In that regard, he was as complicit in Judy's impending ravishment as anyone.

"Women fall in love with me who have never met me," said the Governor. "They write me letters. I have to have someone screen my mail, so I can say I've never seen them."

"Oh, I get letters," said Joe. "And outrageous propositions. In a hotel elevator once – but it doesn't matter. It's the money that makes that happen."

"Money and power," said Shiva.

"Power even more than money, I suspect," said the Governor.

"You know," said Joe, "I'd actually prefer it if the girl said, 'Look, I'll do my best to satisfy you, but I am primarily interested in you because you're rich. That will be a hundred million dollars, please.'"

Shiva laughed. "Is that your going rate?"

"Yeah," said Joe, looking momentarily embarrassed.

"Well, I don't have a hundred million dollars," said the Governor.

Nor do I, said Andrew to himself.

"All I can offer is a little slice of fame, a little piece of George. And the smart ones realise that I am taking a risk with my career, which counts as courage, which is also an aphrodisiac. Or I used to do that. I'm a good boy now."

"He *is* going to run for President," said Shiva, turning to Andrew.

They all laughed.

Venetia of the bathtub had looked out for Andrew all that

shooting party weekend. She explained the jokes. She stood beside him in a clearing in the woods as pheasants flew over them. She gave him enough instruction on the use of a shotgun that he was able to bring down a dozen of the birds – and told the hostess he was "a natural." Best of all, she adopted a pensive manner that convinced everyone they were having wonderful sex, which gave him standing with the other men, which had presumably been his assignment. "That American you sent us did very well," he could imagine important Francis telling the man who ran his firm's London office.

Pretending to be in love had been quite pleasant until the last night, when he started to cry. He had not intended to do that.

"Oh, my sweet American," said Venetia. "What has happened to you?"

"I want to be unfaithful," he stammered, "and I wish I didn't."

"How perfectly awful," she said. "Not wanting something you want. To quote my sainted mother, how did America manage to help us win the war? You couldn't even join the fight until Pearl Harbor."

"Pity you can't meet my mother. She might have sorted you out. She died when I was fourteen. In her world, sleeping with your best friend's husband was *expected* – like knowing how to ride."

"Do you know how to ride?"

"No. When my mother got sick – but it's a long story."

They lay in bed in silence, holding onto each other.

"I'm an American," said Andrew, "as you noted. I believe love is serious." It sounded impolite after he'd said it.

"So why are you in bed with me? We don't even know

each other."

"You've been awfully nice to me," he said.

Venetia was silent too for a few minutes. She stroked the back of his neck as he buried his head in a pillow and recovered his poise. "Of course it's serious," she said finally. "The only way to survive is to make it a game."

Just for a moment, it occurred to Andrew that Rosemary could be playing a game. She was English, after all. And Andrew was a sweet American. Not a confidence-inducing thought.

Janis returned with a tray of drinks. "This one's actually got gin in it," she said, handing one of the glasses to Joe.

And to Andrew: "Cathy says if everyone's come down, it's time to start cooking the lobsters and the steak."

"I'm here," said Rosemary, coming into the living room.

"But what about Cynthia?" said Andrew.

"She'll be here when she gets here," said Joe. "Time to execute some lobsters."

"Let me help," said George.

"I should make myself useful," said Janis.

"Too many cooks," said Andrew, not getting up.

"Yes, sit down," said Shiva, who had made no move to stand up. "I want to know how you know Judy."

"From working for the Governor," she said, following Shiva's suggestion and sitting on the sofa. "I'd been in his office for two years and a bit when one day he asked would I mind sharing my office with someone. 'A young woman with a lot of talent,' he said, 'who could use an older sister.' She showed up the following Monday. She slept on my couch for a couple of weeks until she found her own apartment."

"Nice of you to take her in," said Shiva.

"She's easy to like," said Janis. "Her move from Washington

was sort of thrust upon her. Her Justice called her in one day and said, essentially, 'Here's what you're doing next.'"

"The Governor knows the Justice?" said Shiva.

"The Governor knows everyone."

"Nice to be looked out for," said Andrew.

"She deserves it," said Janis.

"And who looks out for you, Janis?" said Shiva.

"I was raised to be self-reliant," said Janis, standing up. "Excuse me, if you will. I've remembered that I need to find Judy."

That left Andrew sitting in silence with Shiva, sipping their gin-less gin and tonics. "Nice girl," said the Indian finally. "It's a shame George wants to be President."

9

What happened next was shocking, but not entirely a surprise. Life could be like that, Andrew had found. The long rhythms of existence are always there. When Andrew saw Cynthia coming down the stairs ten minutes later, he knew there would be trouble.

She was dressed too well, for one thing. With jewellery. She was determined not to understand what sort of party it was. She stumbled on the second-last step. Andrew reckoned she was thinking about too many things at once. She had a distracted look to her face. Seeing Andrew, she covered it with her mask of innocence. "Have I made us late?" she asked.

"We had to start cooking without you, I'm afraid," said Sally, coming in the door. "The fire wouldn't wait."

"Watch out," said Joe.

They were carrying in a bucket of lobsters and a platter of steak. Andrew was holding the screen door open. Cynthia had contrived to block their path. The Governor took her by the shoulders and moved her out of the way without comment. "Is there more for me to bring in?" George said to Sally.

"I think Janis has the last of the lobsters, but if you'd check, that would be great. And make sure the fire is, you know, behaving itself."

"The fire is fine," said Joe, as he disappeared into the kitchen.

Andrew could see that Cynthia hadn't liked being moved out of the way. He would almost have said she hadn't liked being touched, even by a Governor, even by a political rock star, but his train of thought was interrupted by the sound of breaking glass, followed by Rosemary cursing and Judy telling her not to try to pick up the pieces. "Just back out carefully," said the younger woman in a friendly voice. "You shouldn't try to clean up broken glass barefoot, I think."

"No great loss," Sally called out, presumably to Andrew but for Rosemary's benefit. "Three glasses, it looks like. We tried to put too much on the counter."

Cynthia and Rosemary both retired to the living room, where Shiva and Andrew were sitting, but didn't speak. "Have you made a mess, my darling?" he said to his wife.

"I was trying to make room for the last two platters," she said.

"Perhaps you should put on some shoes," he said.

"Good idea," she said.

Andrew followed her into the kitchen. He wondered if anyone saw her go through the pantry to the maid's room, rather than upstairs, to retrieve them. George brought in the last of the lobsters, for which Judy made room without further damage. "Everyone please fill up a plate and sit down," said Sally, dishing out corn on the cob and sliced tomatoes. "Andrew, would you ask Shiva and Cynthia to come get some dinner?"

Four men and five women is tricky. If you want symmetry, you can put the hostess at the head of the table and go boy-girl-boy-girl down each side. In theory, the hostess is in charge of any dinner table. Andrew thought maybe he didn't want to put Sally in that spot. Janis would look very good there, but he doubted she'd want the role. Part of her shtick was being invisible. Rosemary would look too good. Judy had too much on her mind. Princess Cynthia would probably like being head girl, but that would annoy Rosemary. Also, she hadn't come downstairs yet when Andrew was contemplating seating arrangements.

You know how to do this, he'd said to himself, and extracting a pad and pencil from a drawer in the sideboard, scribbled a chart:

GEORGE

ROSEMARY   CYNTHIA

JOE

ANDREW

SALLY

JUDY   JANIS

SHIVA

This put Andrew in the middle. He was a professional intermediary, after all. It gave the seats of honour to a Governor and a prince, in case anyone cared about protocol. Joe clearly didn't. He'd like sitting next to Sally. Janis could help Judy if she lost her nerve. If Cynthia was a no-show, Sally could take her spot and the table would be symmetrical again. And if Cyn came to dinner but was in a bad mood, Andrew could pay lots of attention to her. And this is high finance? he'd said to himself with a chuckle.

In the end, though, the *placement* couldn't have mattered. Andrew tried to engage Cynthia as soon as everyone sat down, but she paid no attention. What was Shiva going to eat, she wanted to know in a loud voice. The walk they'd gone on evidently hadn't made them friends.

"Everything," he said happily. Not being friends with a skinny celebrity was not something he worried about.

"But isn't that against your religion?" said Cynthia.

"I'm a multi-cultural person," he said. "I honour the customs of the place. I am in magical Nantucket – thanks to Andrew. I have visited a lighthouse – thanks to Joe. I have walked on the beach with a half-naked woman – thanks to your excellent self. And now I will eat beef and lobster – thanks to Cathy and Joe."

This speech made everyone except Cynthia laugh. "So you're a fake Hindu?" she said.

"Hinduism is a syncretic faith," he said. "We have many gods and many customs."

The Governor of Massachusetts interrupted: "I move that eating strange foods be viewed as tolerance rather than misbehaviour."

"How about kissing strange women?" Judy blurted out and then looked at her lap.

"Uh...indeed," said the Governor. He paused. "And in that spirit, I propose a toast to our host and hostess." He reached for his glass, which was empty. Rosemary poured him some wine from one of the bottles Sally had put on the table. "Not too much, please," he said.

"I'm not drinking at all," said Cynthia. It seemed to Andrew that alcohol was exactly what Cynthia needed, but he didn't want to start an argument.

"I will follow the Governor's gracious suggestion," said Shiva. Janis poured him half a glass.

"To new friends and old," said the Governor, raising his glass and looking around the table.

"I'll vote for him," said Joe.

Again, everyone except Cynthia laughed. But suddenly everyone was talking at once, and it didn't matter. "How do you open this thing?" said Shiva, pointing to his lobster.

"You use the cracker," said Judy. "Let me show you." She held her hand around his and applied pressure until the claw broke open. He liked that.

"You put the shells in the empty bowls," said Sally.

"Where's the melted butter?" said Janis.

"It must still be in the kitchen," said Sally.

"I'll get it," said Janis.

Cynthia hadn't engaged with her crustacean yet. She doesn't do messy, Andrew said to himself. He looked over at Rosemary and saw that she was reading his mind.

"I forgot to buy bibs," said Sally.

"It doesn't matter," said Rosemary.

"Just to remind everyone," said Sally, "there's one apiece with three left over."

"After that you have to make do with steak," said Joe.

"It is pretty impressive steak," said the Governor, acknowledging Joe's contribution. "I assume you eat steak," he said to Cynthia, "coming from Texas."

"If someone wants my lobster..." she said.

"That makes it one and a half each," said Judy, who was getting enthusiastically messy.

"You have lobster expertise, I see," said Shiva.

"Do you come from Nantucket?" said Cynthia.

"Boston," said Judy. "North End. Grew up in sight of the Old North Church. As in Paul Revere and the midnight ride. Do you know that poem? Henry Wadsworth Longfellow. Don't you wish you had a grand name like that?"

"I know that bit of American history," said Shiva. "And the Governor does have that sort of name, in case you've forgotten."

"Shiva's full name takes five minutes to say," said Rosemary, "but you're not allowed to say it all because some bits are sacred."

"She's making that up," said Shiva, smiling at his wife. She tilted her head a bit. "Well, mostly making it up," he said.

"I'll bet Lady Rosemary is good at making things up," said the Governor. She accepted the compliment by looking down as if demurely.

"The North End's an Italian neighbourhood now," said Judy, expertly extracting meat from her lobster's skinny legs. "Good restaurants but no Longfellows."

"What does your father do?" said Cynthia.

She probably thinks he's a garbage collector, Andrew said to himself. She appeared to be looking for a fight.

"I don't know," said Judy. "He disappeared before I was born, according to my mother. Late mother, I should say."

"So you're illegitimate," said Cynthia. She didn't want a fight. She wanted a car crash. But Judy refused to oblige her by reacting. Andrew envied her confidence.

"Did she get to see you graduate from law school and become a Supreme Court clerk?" said Rosemary, pretending not to hear Cynthia.

"She did," said Judy. "But only because I went to college when I was fifteen. I got a scholarship. She died right before I moved back to Boston. I came home for the funeral and when I got back to Washington I learned that I was going back to

Boston. That's why I had to sleep on Janis's couch. I couldn't face living where she died. I don't believe in ghosts, except that maybe I do."

"Call them 'spirits,'" said Shiva.

"She must have been very proud," said the Governor softly.

"Does it bother you, Judy, being a bastard?" said Cynthia in her innocent interviewer voice. She's unhinged, Andrew said to himself. He wondered why Joe didn't try to rein her in.

"Being illegitimate is not a person's fault," said the Governor. "Used to be, but society is kinder than it was even twenty-five years ago."

"It wasn't always a bad deal," said Rosemary.

She was trying to take the spotlight off Judy, Andrew could see, same as George. Of course, whatever Cynthia's problem was, it had nothing to do with Judy.

"I'm descended from a bastard myself," said Rosemary, "one of a dozen or more with whom Charles the Second endowed his kingdom. My great, great, great, however many it is, grandmother. His Majesty married her off to the son of one of the nobles who had accompanied him to France."

"So are you a Roman Catholic?" said Janis.

"Well, I probably should be, but I'm not. I was christened that way but I've missed confession too often to claim affiliation."

"Can we assume you've had plenty to confess?" said Cynthia, but no one paid attention to her.

"My mother was a Roman Catholic," said Judy. "She went to mass every morning before she went to work. She was a secretary."

"What did she pray for?" said Cynthia. It struck Andrew that she actually wanted to know the answer.

"I think she prayed for me," said Judy, answering Cynthia

127

in a surprisingly gentle voice. "And for my father."

"Did she tell you that?" said the Governor.

"No," said Judy. "She wouldn't tell me anything about him. But it would have been like her to pray for him. She was a charitable person."

"And so are you," said the Governor.

Andrew looked over at Rosemary again. She nodded her head in Cynthia's direction. The woman appeared to be working up to something. Now we will have that car crash, he told himself.

"I've made an interesting discovery," said Cynthia to no one in particular.

"What's that?" said Judy in a friendly voice. *See what I told you about her being charitable?* George's face said.

"Pictures in frames," said Cynthia. The hairs on the back of Andrew's neck stood up. "In the drawer at the bottom of the linen closet." Sally looked up. "Pictures of your family, Andrew." Everyone had stopped talking. "Pictures of you and two girls who look like you and a woman who isn't here."

"That would be Cathy," said Sally, with astonishing aplomb. Looking around the table, Andrew realised that everyone except Cynthia already knew his wife had gone missing. He should have told Sally that. Fortunately – Rosemary had.

"Now that we know you aren't Andrew's wife," Cynthia continued, "perhaps we should know who you are?"

"Does it matter?" said Rosemary.

"I think she's a very nice hostess," said Shiva.

"How can we say it doesn't matter?" said Cynthia. "We've been lied to. We've been here under false pretences – or invited under false pretences. Andrew said, quote, he and Cathy were inviting us. Come stay with us on Nantucket, he said."

"Cathy and I did invite you," said Andrew, "but when we arrived, she'd gone missing."

"If it's anyone's fault, it's mine," said Sally. "My name is 'Sally' if you care. But I wasn't the point of the weekend, and neither was Cathy, to be fair. So I suggested to Andrew that we just pretend I was Cathy. He had about fifteen seconds to decide what to do."

"At the airport," said Joe.

"Pretty gutsy move," said Janis. Andrew liked her saying that.

"But I mean," said Cynthia, "you had to sleep together."

"Men and women do that," said Rosemary.

"We had to disappear into the same bedroom," said Sally. "That's all."

"Well, it gives me the creeps," said Cynthia. "What's happened to the real Cathy? Have you murdered her?"

"Perhaps," said Andrew, feeling briefly mischievous. "But no, we don't know where she is."

"I told Andrew she'd gone to Munich to see their older daughter, Eleanor. I said she was having some sort of emotional crisis."

"Eleanor's been having an emotional crisis for several months," said Andrew, "so I believed it. And to be honest, I wasn't particularly worried. She's twenty. Eleanor is, I mean. She doesn't know what she wants to do with her life. Her younger sister has a serious boyfriend and she doesn't. So she's decided she hates her parents – or at least her father."

"We don't hate you, Andrew," said Janis.

"Thank you. And I assume Eleanor is just going through a phase."

"But doesn't it bother you to be hated?" said Judy.

"After twenty years on Wall Street, I can cope with hostility."

"After half a century in my beloved but complicated family, I understand the concept," said Shiva. "Not that it doesn't sometimes require fortitude."

"Indeed," said the Governor. "Nearly half the people of Massachusetts vote against me."

"Only forty per cent of those who voted," said Janis, "which means less than a quarter of the adult population."

"Janis looks after my ego as well as my office," said the Governor.

"A good quality in a woman," said Shiva.

"But not necessarily good for the man," said Rosemary.

"The point is," said Andrew, "I thought I knew where Cathy was, but it wasn't relevant. I'd invited Joe and Shiva here, with their beautiful wives – he smiled at Rosemary and then at Cynthia, with mixed results – to get to know each other, not to know Cathy and me."

"But we've *enjoyed* getting to know you, Andrew," said Rosemary.

That was something of an understatement, which Andrew hoped Rosemary planned to elaborate on later that night. He managed to suppress his own smile.

"And we've liked getting to know you too, Sally," she continued, "even if you turned out not to be Cathy." Rosemary had definitely warned Sally she'd been found out. She could have done that while he and Joe were building the fire. Or at the whaling museum while Joe looked at every exhibit.

"So you lied to Andrew too," said Cynthia, ignoring the general laughter at Rosemary's remarks.

"I did," said Sally, "but that was simpler than telling Andrew I didn't know where she'd gone. Or perhaps I should say 'more expedient.' I didn't want to distract him."

The thought briefly visited Andrew that Sally was telling him she knew where Cathy was, but he ignored it. He'd be told when he needed to know. "I *would* have been distracted," he said. And of course Sally knew.

"Cathy – I mean Sally – did what any good subordinate would do," said Joe. "I for one appreciate it, and I imagine Shiva does too. We had an agenda this weekend." Andrew watched Joe think about what he'd just said and turn towards Sally. "Not that you're anyone's subordinate," he corrected himself.

"Employee," said Sally, smiling at Joe.

"It's what wives do, Cynthia," said Rosemary. "You'll come to understand that eventually."

The beautiful Texan turned her head as if she'd been slapped. She knows she's failing as Joe's "missus," Andrew said to himself.

"I told you when you arrived in the third form," Rosemary continued, suddenly on the attack. "'You are not a princess.' We had *actual* princesses at St. Elizabeth's, but even they weren't allowed to carry on like princesses. Remember?"

"Did you two go to school together?" said Janis. "Why didn't you mention it before?"

"I didn't bring it up because St. Elizabeth's was a painful experience for Cynthia."

"She was awful to me," said Cynthia. "She made me stand on a pile of books barefoot."

This made Joe laugh. "Maybe I should try that," he said.

"Careful," said Rosemary. "It was a very tough year."

"Were they difficult books?" said Shiva.

Rosemary gave her husband a sharp look. Having seized the upper hand, she didn't need to destroy her former schoolmate.

"It didn't matter what the books were about," said Cynthia. Andrew realised she was close to crying. "It was a punishment. It was unfair. The hall where you had to do it was cold. Everyone could look at you. The books wobbled. You had to stand there for half an hour, and if you fell off you had to start again."

"What was the punishment for?" said Joe. It was clear he had never heard about this chapter in his wife's life before. It was also obvious that the notion of "punishment" interested him.

"It was a punishment for being an American," said Cynthia. "I was an exchange student. I was fourteen. I was homesick. *Lady* Rosemary was head prefect. She could do anything she wanted." Cynthia paused to gather her strength. "And I desperately wanted her to like me. You were smart. You were beautiful…"

"I was not a nice person," Rosemary interrupted. "Sadly still true. But you are not correct that I could do anything I wanted. There were rules. You were being punished for complaining, which St. Elizabeth's regarded as a cardinal sin. I had no choice about the matter, even if I had reciprocated your crush, which I didn't."

"The food was awful. The house was cold. We had to play stupid games in the mud and pretend we liked them."

"All good training," said Sally.

"What would you know about that?" hissed Cynthia, her anger boiling over at a stranger's intervention.

"I've worked as a nanny," said Sally. "In the past, that is."

"And what do you do now," said Cynthia, "if I may ask."

"I'm a prostitute."

Reactions to this statement spilled out on top of each other.

"Party girl," George corrected her. If Sally and the

Governor already knew each other, it explained the way she'd greeted him that afternoon.

Cynthia more or less snorted. I knew that, she seemed to be saying.

"How exciting," said Judy.

"And I suppose you didn't know that," said Cynthia to Andrew in a sarcastic voice.

"I did not," said Andrew. There was no point in arguing with her. She'd eagerly undressed for Shiva earlier in the day, and now she was claiming to be offended – same as when Janis and Judy showed up. Cynthia, the prudish nude, he said to himself. Or was it nudish prude? Perhaps he needed to slow down on the wine.

"What a stunt," said Shiva, "if I may use that word." He appeared to assume Andrew had indeed arranged it.

Janis gave nothing away.

"Still working?" said Rosemary, as if she and pretend Cathy were colleagues.

"Not as such," said Sally. "I stopped ten years ago. But I've always felt it would be dishonest to pretend I wasn't in the profession when I unquestionably had been in my twenties. Once a whore…"

Sally paused, as if what came next was the important revelation. "I was also a dominatrix for a while."

Joe started to laugh and then suppressed it.

"Mostly I found *that* depressing," Sally continued. "You work out what your client wants, and it's obviously painful. You're touching something deep inside him. There ought to be healing going on. But next week or next month he's back exactly the same, all eager to be hurt again. I don't know how psychoanalysts stand it. I had to quit. But it taught me a lot about people."

"So what do you do now?" said Rosemary. "And how did whatever her name is, Andrew's wife, find you?"

"You might say I'm a party planner. I get hired to make interesting things happen. When I was a domme, as I said, I discovered I could tell what people wanted…"

"What men wanted?" said Rosemary. By this point everyone else had stopped talking and was listening to this conversation.

"Men and women both. I come as a guest but partway through the party, I get things started."

Perhaps it was in that context that George had encountered Sally. Andrew hoped so anyway. One cannot help wanting to know the President, and campaigns tend to uncover any damaging secrets a candidate has. But Andrew doubted his friend enjoyed being spanked.

"The objective is to let people have what they want but could never admit to," Sally continued.

"You pretend to be a normal guest," said Janis. "Just one who nobody else has met before. That's what you said, isn't it? The hostess introduces you as if you were a friend from out of town."

"That's right," said Sally. "If I'm identified as a professional party-starter – that's a better name for it than party planner – if they know what I am, it makes people self-conscious."

"It isn't making me self-conscious," said Joe.

"But *you* never are," said Cynthia.

"So what do *we* want?" said Rosemary.

"I want another lobster," said Sally cheerfully, standing up. By Andrew's count there were two of them left. "Anyone else?"

"What about my steak?" said Joe.

Sally gave him a smile and disappeared into the kitchen.

10

For a long moment, Sally having disappeared, the rest of the group just looked at each other. They all knew there was more. We're like primitive tribesmen about to be initiated, Andrew said to himself – adolescents waiting in the dark, waiting to confront the monster, hoping to withstand the rumoured pain, hoping to have a vision and become adults. It was a magical island. Sally had declared herself to have magical powers. She could divine secrets. At some level, everyone wanted to believe her.

"So what *does* everyone want?" said Rosemary, breaking the silence.

"I want to sleep with your husband," said Judy gleefully, "but you already know that."

"Is that all right with you, Shiva?" said Rosemary, as if she were asking him to give Judy a ride into town. "I should have mentioned it before. But this young American is so sweet and eager. Perhaps some of your sophistication will rub off on her. She's going to be a famous judge some day, I understand, probably a Supreme Court justice. She needs to become worldly. She is like a crown princess who will one day be the ruler. She needs instruction. Could you manage that?"

At first, Shiva looked embarrassed, but as Rosemary spoke, the way she expressed the proposition began to tickle him. "I accept," he said to Judy. He would have known what was afoot, of course, seeing her clothes in his closet. And then, turning to Janis, as if she had a say in what happened to her friend: "Is that all right? Do you approve?"

"You have my blessing," said Janis.

Shiva took up Janis's hand and kissed it. Janis blushed. She was less sure of her footing than she looked. Andrew liked her blushing.

"Andrew," said Rosemary. "Do we have any more champagne?" He rose from his chair. "And while you're up, could you bring out whatever's left of dinner?"

"Of course," said Andrew. As he went to the kitchen, he passed Sally, who was returning to the table. He avoided catching her eye. He wasn't sure what relationship they were now supposed to have.

"Judy, you're out of the game," said Rosemary, assuming the role of hostess now that Sally had become a shaman, "so perhaps you could empty the bowls with the lobster shells and bring them back. Joe, if you expect to sell any of your steak, you'd better get the platter."

When everyone had claimed whatever food they wanted, Rosemary picked up the thread of the conversation. "So, Cathy – I think we'll keep calling you that – what comes next?"

"Why should we call her Cathy?" said Cynthia, her rage undiminished. "She isn't Cathy. She's an imposter."

"As it happens, I know the other Cathy," said the Governor, sticking his forefinger deep into the tail of the last lobster to extract the meat. "She's a nice girl. A bit frosty, sometimes. Isn't that right, Andrew?"

Andrew had a mouth full of steak and chose not to respond.

"But this Cathy is a very good understudy," the Governor continued, "and perhaps more fun than the original. Enthusiastic hostess. I think we should thank her for her efforts, treat her with appropriate respect."

Cynthia made a guttural dismissive noise.

"I think we should call them *both* 'Cathy,'" said Shiva. "Neither one is the *real* Cathy or the *other* Cathy. They are simply different manifestations of a single reality. But perhaps I am thinking like a Hindu. In Puritan New England, one does not manifest, as I recall."

The Governor smiled. "One does," he said, "but not everyone is comfortable with it. The Puritans turned into Unitarians."

"What *are* you two talking about?" said Cynthia.

"Boys showing off," said Rosemary.

"I want to know more about this party-starting business," said Joe, whose interest in metaphysics was limited.

"Or is '*games* mistress' a better term?" said Rosemary.

"I like that," said Shiva, smiling at his wife. And then to Andrew: "A woman of manifest wit, is she not?"

Andrew had the sudden sense that Shiva was essentially presenting him with Rosemary, which probably told him all he needed to know about their marriage. You may have her, he seemed to be saying. Her clothes have left my closet. I understand. But please appreciate her. Acknowledge what an extraordinary woman I have collected, and now give to you. Andrew definitely appreciated Rosemary. But she'd given herself away, actually. All Shiva had done was let go – and he'd done that years earlier.

Cynthia had said, at some point, back when she was trying to flirt with Shiva, and he had referred to Nantucket as a "magical island," that a happy marriage was a magical island. Shiva had responded that the quest for a happy marriage was misguided. His mother had told him that. What you wanted, she had said, was a "successful" marriage. Which perhaps he and Lady Rosemary had achieved. Andrew wished he could be sure Judy understood that.

"So you persuade adults to play spin-the-bottle?" said Cynthia, still trying to pick a fight. "Is that what you do, *Cathy the Second*?" She glanced at Shiva as she said this.

"If that's all they're up to," said Sally.

"I take it your job is to get people to do things they don't want to do," said Cynthia. "That's what our games mistress did at St. Elizabeth's. She made us be cold and get muddy." She seemed covertly interested in what Sally was saying.

"No," said Joe. "She gets people to do things they *do* want to do, but are reluctant to propose." He looked over at his wife. She avoided eye contact.

"You mean if I'm being a very *strict* games mistress?" said Sally.

"Um," said Joe. The notion that he liked "strict" stood out all over him. This was a man who could conjure hundreds of millions of dollars out of the air by apprehending reality ahead of his competitors. But privately, he liked fantasies.

"Do you do strict?" said Rosemary.

"I can. But the point is not what I do but what my clients do to each other, once they're given permission."

"Proceed," said Rosemary grandly.

"Well, here's something I've done a few times – and to be clear, I'm not proposing it." She paused while the last lobster shells were tossed into bowls and wine glasses were recharged. "It's moderately naughty," Sally continued. "Moderately dastardly in fact. Could I have another glass of wine too, please, Andrew sweetheart?"

She was going into character, Andrew realised, which was a bit nervous-making. His guests were gleefully expectant. If this were a primitive festival, Andrew would be the sacrificial pig. Not fat, you understand – Andrew still looked fine in a swimming suit – just destined for butchering.

"I use this game when there are two women at a party who are quarrelling," said Sally.

"As you and Cynthia seem to be," said Janis.

"Or rivals or enemies," said Sally, "though maybe they don't admit it. But I hope Cynthia doesn't regard me that way." She smiled at the group, having ensured that Cynthia would hate her, at least for present purposes.

"We can be enemies if you want," said Cynthia defiantly.

"As you like," said Sally. "It's called the husband game. Here's how it works. The two women…"

"You and me," said Cynthia.

Yes, butchering, Andrew said to himself.

"We can play if you like," said Sally. "The way it starts is that we make our husbands undress."

Sharp intake of breath.

"But you don't have a husband," said Judy.

"Andrew was my husband yesterday. And Joe is still Cynthia's, I think. They'll do."

Andrew looked over at Joe, who shrugged. He realised Joe would be perfectly comfortable naked. Good body. Probably liked the idea. Andrew himself didn't like the idea, but he was trapped. He was responsible for Sally's presence. He was entertaining billionaires. He had to play whatever games were proposed.

"Then each of the women…"

"Do we want to know this?" said Rosemary, interrupting.

"Of course we do," said Shiva.

"We could all just *imagine* what comes next," said Rosemary. "The reality could be quite ugly. We could have Caliban at the door." No one spoke. She had Andrew's vote but evidently no one else's. "Go ahead if you all want to," she said.

"It's quite simple, really," Sally continued. "Each of the women attempts to excite the other one's husband."

The Governor chuckled. He might have met Sally before, but this was new.

"The woman who brings the process to a conclusion first is the winner," said Sally, "and gets to give her enemy or rival or competitor, whatever I'm supposed to call you" – she looked at Cynthia – "a good spanking." She paused and let the thought sink in. "Are you good at spanking, Cynthia?" she asked.

"Not really," said Joe. "I mean, to be honest, I don't think Cyn would like this game."

"Try me," said Cynthia.

"OK," said Joe. He had no problem with the game. That was clear. And no problem with what got done to his current wife. Her hundred-million-dollar cheque had already been written.

"House rules?" said Sally.

"Meaning what?" said Cynthia.

"How long is the spanking?"

"Five minutes?" said Cynthia.

"It gets old within two minutes," said Sally. "For both parties."

"Two minutes, then."

"Let's get on with it," said Sally calmly.

Joe began to unbutton his shirt without further instruction. Andrew did the same.

"Is this sophistication?" said Judy.

"Depravity, actually," said Rosemary. "Something you need to know about."

Once you *decide* you are going to undress, Andrew discovered, it gets easier. You have permission. He sat down on a chair and took off his shoes, then stood up and took off his chino trousers. The shock is when you first *realise* you're going to do it.

"When do we start?" said Cynthia.

"We already have," said Sally.

Sally walked around Joe like someone who'd just bought a Ferrari. "Really nice rear end," she said, running two fingers down Joe's spine. "Since you're all new at this game, I should point out that not thinking about sex is quite important."

"I get it," said Janis, interrupting.

"Go on then," said Sally.

"Well, the deal is," said Janis, "each of you is counting on your husband being unaffected by your competitor's... ministrations. A good husband would make it his business to be impervious."

"But as the good husband watches his wife attending to the other man," said the Governor, picking up the thread, "he sees his wife in a new light, which possibly turns him on." George looked briefly embarrassed. "It might turn some men on," he said.

"Which means his poor wife will get spanked," said Janis. "Oh, I like this game."

"You do?" said Judy.

"Well, a bit." Janis liked the idea of George's wife Lydia getting spanked, Andrew decided. He liked it that she wasn't coy about that.

"And while he wants to be the good husband," said the Governor, "the prospect of his darling wife being spanked..."

"...in front of everyone..." Janis interjected.

"...makes it impossible for him to defend her," said the Governor, "with his continence."

"I think Janis is beginning to relax," said Sally. Janis blushed again.

"Now, there are a lot of ways to go at this," said Sally. "And, Cynthia, you can start on Andrew however and whenever you like. But with such a beautiful bottom as I have available to me here" – she leaned down and took off one of her flat shoes – "I think it's pretty clear what to do."

She struck the aforesaid bottom. Joe gasped – as did most of her audience. She hit him again.

"Ohio somewhere," he said. "You wore a mask. I was buying a company. Little promotional flier in the hotel room. Very coy. Massage can be arranged."

"You gave me a thousand dollar tip."

"Worth every penny," he said.

"I think better of you already, Joe," said Rosemary.

"Leave him in the little world he's in, please," said Sally.

"Of course," said Rosemary. "But do we need to continue?"

"Don't be a spoil-sport," said Shiva.

"Well if you must, at least take the show outside. All four of you. And take your clothes, Andrew."

"But how will we know who wins?" said Joe, a competitor again, as Sally gathered up his discarded garments.

"I suspect that will be easy," said Rosemary, but if we need a referee, George can do the honours. He's a public official, after all."

Both couples went out onto the porch. No actual Caliban visible. Cynthia insisted they locate themselves around the corner from each other. The water-resistant cushions on the porch sofa were cold. The evening breeze dusted Andrew with goose-bumps. Cynthia sat down beside him. "I can't do this," she said quietly. The fight had all gone out of her.

"You'll get spanked," he said.

"I get spanked all the time," she said. Andrew must have registered alarm, because she added quickly, "Oh, not by Joe. By life."

"I wouldn't have thought so," said Andrew. "Joe is – well, it's becoming hard to say what Joe is."

"Joe is a gentleman, actually," said Cynthia, "even if he can be obtuse. It's life that's a bitch."

"Joe gets what he wants," said Andrew.

A whoop from around the corner indicated that he had.

"Which clearly isn't me," said Cynthia. "*Happily* isn't me, to be honest."

The Governor of Massachusetts stuck his head out the door. "Do I need to adjudicate?" he asked.

"We concede," said Andrew. George's head disappeared.

Cynthia stood up and undressed as Andrew did the opposite. "Time to feed the lions," she said, putting on an almost believable smile.

"Why do we do these things?" Andrew asked her. He meant the question in a cosmic sense.

"Loneliness," said Cynthia. "Holding it off, that is."

Sally stopped after the first dozen smacks. Cynthia refused

champagne and went upstairs immediately.

"Oh my," said Judy.

"Yes," said Janis.

"But what does Andrew get for his trouble?" said Shiva. "What's his reward for this, I must say, extraordinary entertainment?"

"He gets his fee letters signed," said Rosemary unexpectedly. "Twenty million from each of you. And you're hiring him personally, not his firm."

"His former firm," said Joe, who seemed unsurprised. "My only proviso is that he abandons any claim on Sally."

"We're just good friends," said Andrew. Sally grinned.

"And if I could ask a favour, Andrew," said Shiva. "Would you keep Rosemary company while I'm away? I may need to visit India..."

"...and Rosemary is tired of curry," said Rosemary.

"It would be an honour," said Andrew.

"It better be more than that," said Rosemary. "But what about Janis?"

"She's going to write up our agreements tomorrow," said Joe, "so I suggest she goes to bed."

"A four-poster bed?" said Sally.

It took several seconds for the Governor to react. "Why not?" he said finally. "Lydia will never believe I'm *not* sleeping with you."

"But where will *you* sleep?" said Janis to Andrew. Nice of her to care.

"We're the help," said Rosemary. "We sleep in the servant's room at the end of the pantry."

Everyone laughed. The complexities of life had vanished in a bonfire of sexual honesty.

"Our revels now are ended?" said Shiva.

"Maybe," said the Governor.

"For now," said Rosemary.

"Good night, Prospero," said Andrew.

11

Andrew woke early, as so often. There was no light yet around the edges of the curtains. Rosemary's head was on his shoulder, her arm across his chest. Her body had the heaviness of sleep. He didn't move. The cello recommenced.

After what could have been half an hour, Rosemary's breathing changed. "Come see the dawn," said Andrew.

"Only if we go to the beach," Rosemary said without lifting her head. "And naked, I expect," said Andrew.

"Should that be in question?" The violins began to dance.

Andrew got out of bed, picked up his red-and-white striped nightshirt, which had spent the night on the floor, gave Rosemary undisputed access to the bathroom, took his turn, brushed his teeth, remembered interrupted love-making.

They'd talked in the darkness. "Your voice is as beautiful as you are," he'd said.

"Don't tell me I'm beautiful," she'd answered softly. "Tell me I'm wise."

"You are wise beyond my comprehension," he'd said. "You saw everything."

"Not quite everything," she said. "I remembered glamorous

Cynthia as skinny fourteen-year-old Cynthia Jane from Texas, a stubborn girl it was my job to train. I never could break her, which I found almost as annoying as her accent. It turns out I misjudged her."

"Poor Joe," said Andrew.

"It's working out just fine for Joe," Rosemary had said. "But I fear Cynthia Jane is only beginning her journey of self-discovery."

For a while they were silent. "I hope it isn't your job to break me," he'd said. Silence bred doubts. Cathy had been good at silent.

"No, my darling," said Rosemary. "No no no. My fate and pleasure is to please you. I knew that as soon as we met in London, at dinner with Shiva at that restaurant with the candles and old silver. You were quoting poetry like an undergraduate, sketching deals I could not understand, trying to persuade a sceptical Indian prince to trust a man he had never met – and unable to stop looking at the prince's wife. I saw right away that you were brave and smart and wounded. You will need a lot of fucking, you know."

"I know."

He'd kissed her. She was good at that. She was good at everything. "In that silly game tonight," she'd said, "thank you for saving yourself for me."

"It wasn't hard," he'd said. "And pretty soon neither was I."

She'd poked him in the ribs. "It was endearing, though," she'd said. "Now come closer."

They touched each other tentatively in silence. "Why would anyone want to be spanked?" he'd asked.

"Strange wiring," said Rosemary, "but it doesn't seem to embarrass Joe." And then: "I'm feeling bad about Cynthia Jane.

Would you just hold me for a while?"

"Of course," Andrew had said, turning and wrapping an arm around Rosemary. Suddenly it seemed important to put space between the savage ceremony Sally had made them part of and what they did in private for each other. Sleep had agreed, laying its soft blanket over them almost immediately. And now it was a new day.

They went downstairs and out the door as quietly as possible. When they got to the tunnel through the bushes, they heard a noise from the house and looking back saw George and Janis, evidently on the same errand. George had always looked good naked. He and Janis looked good together, though it felt impolite to stare at her. "Shall we wait for them?" said Andrew.

"I want to be first," said Rosemary. She danced down the wooden steps and into the shallow surf. Janis was in after her within half a minute, and they began splashing each other. More freckles.

"Did we ever expect this, when we were eighteen?" the Governor asked his old friend, as they watched their women get wet.

"Of course we did," said Andrew, "but this is better. We thought everything was possible then. We thought we were immortal. Now that we know the truth, life is sweeter."

"Sometimes," said the Governor.

"Sometimes," Andrew agreed.

They both knew they were thinking of the missing Cathy, who had pretended to be happy for so many years. And of Lydia, who had taken a vow to be disgruntled. And other misadventures.

Janis and Rosemary came out of the sea, slapping themselves to get warm. "A double date," said George.

"I don't think we ever had one," said Andrew.

Joe and Sally came down the wooden steps and joined the four of them. "Why do people wear clothes?" said Joe. "It seems so unnecessary."

"Shiva would never do this," said Rosemary.

"Nor would Judy," said Janis.

"Except that here they come," said Sally.

"He's not as bad looking as he thinks he is," said Rosemary.

"She's good for him," said Sally.

"I accept that," said Rosemary to Sally.

"You accepted it last night," said Sally. "And rather nicely."

For a moment, everyone, except possibly the Governor, who was watching the horizon become distinct, watched Judy and Shiva approach. "See the brave way she doesn't cover herself, and how he likes that," said Sally.

"One's manners improve with age," said Rosemary finally, in response to Sally's compliment, though mostly to herself.

"Oh, I hope that's true," said Judy, having joined them.

"Do you know what we were talking about?" said Sally.

"No idea," said Judy. "I agree with everyone this morning." And then, as if it were a matter she had been asked to investigate: "Sex is astonishing."

"The sun's about to rise," said the Governor.

For a long minute they all looked east in silence, hugging their new partners, letting the earth revolve.

"I liked that," said Sally, speaking to Joe but also to them all. "Being held tightly at dawn."

"Special occasion," said Rosemary.

"She mostly does moonlight," said Shiva.

"I'm changing my ways," said Rosemary.

"I'm retiring," said Shiva.

"You are?" said Joe, pleased but clearly surprised.

"Hadn't I mentioned that?" said Shiva. He sounded like Rosemary suggesting he take Judy to see a tiger. "I want you to run the whole thing – not just the company Andrew is making us invent, but also my whole empire. It will make the tax authorities unable to attack Andrew's structure. It simplifies everything, in fact. This way, you and I won't have to spend three months on the shareholders' agreement. This way, I'll never have to argue with my brothers again. Can you do that for me? I will pay you a dollar a year."

Joe laughed.

"He isn't kidding," said Judy.

"Your idea?" said Rosemary.

"Partly," said Judy. "You said he needed a vacation, and I said to myself, why not a long vacation?"

"And Janis will write it all up this morning," said Shiva, "having had a good night's sleep."

"Along with the fee agreements and the confidentiality agreement regarding last night's activities," said Janis.

"Is a confidentiality agreement necessary?" said Joe.

"It needs to have nine signatures," said the Governor.

"Umm," said Andrew.

There was a brief silence.

"Is she up yet?" said Janis. "Did anyone hear her moving in her bedroom?"

"Evidently not," said Sally.

"You don't suppose she would have killed herself?" said Rosemary.

"Rosemary!" said Andrew.

"Very badly brought up," said Shiva.

"But honest," said Rosemary.

150

"I was having the same thought," said Janis.

"What I think we should do," said the Governor, "and before some citizen with an iPhone discovers the eight of us looking like a sequel to *Lord of the Flies,* is go back and make pancakes and be very nice to the Emmy-winning Cynthia McAllister."

"Oh, God, I forgot she was a journalist," said Andrew.

"I suspect *she* forgot," said Joe.

"She did get rather carried away," said Janis.

"But to no effect," said Rosemary, smiling slyly at Andrew.

"Um, yes," said Andrew. "Let's be *very* nice to Cynthia."

"She'd be implicating herself, if she wanted to spill the beans," said Janis.

"She wouldn't like the publicity," said Joe. "Her audience wouldn't like it, is what she'd say."

"*Lots* of pancakes," said the Governor.

The eight of them started back for the stairs. "I think we look like a painting," said Judy happily. "One of those French paintings…"

"Goddesses and warriors," said Andrew.

"Flashing breastplates and diaphanous gowns," said Sally.

"Fabulous vistas," said the Governor, enjoying the way Judy had triggered everyone's imagination, "and puffy white clouds."

"That's just what I meant," said Judy.

The house was full of the smell of bacon frying. Cynthia was in the kitchen attending to it on the stove's built-in griddle. She seemed a different person. Her hair was pulled back and tied with a sky-blue ribbon. She was wearing nothing but a long black apron, with "Rome, Paris, Nantucket" in large white letters down the front. "When the fat splatters, it hurts," she explained.

"Of course," said Rosemary sympathetically.

"I looked out an upstairs window and saw you all leaving. Nudity seemed to be the uniform of the day." Definitely a new day, Andrew said to himself. Whatever demons had possessed Cynthia the previous evening seemed to have been exorcised.

"I burn," said Rosemary. "I have to put on clothes before the sun gets any higher. I hope the rest of you will join me so I won't be self-conscious."

"Oh, all right," said Joe.

"I'll finish the bacon first," said Cynthia. "Then the men can do the pancakes."

Andrew followed Rosemary into the servant's room to get dressed. "Do you think he knows?" said Rosemary.

"Are you thinking what I am?"

"Regarding Judy?" said Rosemary.

"Yes to all your questions. You can see it in the way he speaks to her, the way he *doesn't* look at her."

"Do you think *she* knows?" said Rosemary.

"I'd say not. Janis says she's a blurter, and there hasn't been a hint."

"Do you think he's going to say anything? Do you think he wants to? You know him better."

"He wants to but he won't," said Andrew. "He hasn't yet. For a man with his reputation, he's remarkably self-disciplined."

"He funded her scholarships?"

"Unquestionably."

"Should we do anything?"

"If a deal is meant to happen, it will happen," said Andrew. To be honest, he didn't know the answer to Rosemary's question.

"Time to make pancakes," she said.

The thing about pancakes, Andrew reminded himself, is

that you can't make enough for everyone at once, so there have to be people eating while others have nothing. So there is the issue of what order people get served in. If people are polite, they won't sit down because that amounts to asking to be served ahead of others, so there is a lot of milling around. Needless to say, assigning seats is impossible.

Rosemary extracted a large carving knife from the knife block and began cutting oranges in half. Joe had bought dozens. Sally began pushing them down on the electric squeezer. Janis started setting the table.

Joe appeared and started reading the instructions on the box of pancake batter. "I happen to be good at making pancakes," he said.

"He is," said Cynthia, coming in. "And good at eating them." For the first time all weekend, she looked like she was on holiday. "I'll mix, you pour and flip." She searched under the counter and found a bowl.

"You've done your part with the bacon," said Joe. "Pancakes are men's work."

"Eggs are in the refrigerator," said Sally. "Maple syrup's in the pantry."

"Should we warm the plates?" said Judy.

"That's always a good idea," said George.

"Plates are still in the dishwasher," said Sally. "Shiva, out of the way. You do not belong in a kitchen."

"No, he doesn't," said Rosemary. Shiva backed off as far as the door, but everyone wanted to be in the kitchen, it appeared.

As Joe produced pancakes, three plates of three at a go, Andrew handed them out. "If you're fast," he said to Joe, "we may eventually get everyone sitting down at once. I sense that Cynthia wants to say something."

"I agree with you," said Joe, hurrying up. "Let's see if we can get enough done to sit down ourselves."

The tide of people and second helpings flowed back and forth. Joe piled up a final platter. He and Andrew took the last of the plates out of the oven and went in. As people will, most of his guests had returned to the seats they'd occupied the night before, but Cynthia had elected to sit next to Sally, displacing Judy, who hadn't decided where to go.

If truth wants to manifest itself it will. "Here," said Andrew, pulling out the chair between himself and the Governor, "sit next to your father."

He'd been thinking about Eleanor, he told Rosemary later. "I was distracted. Being hated is painful," he explained.

"She doesn't hate you," said Rosemary. "It's just displacement activity from some other issue. Anger often is."

"You're a wise woman," Andrew told her, earning a quick smile. She knew what he was doing but she still liked it.

But that was later. Andrew's unplanned announcement made Judy gasp; for a moment she appeared shocked and confused, but then she smiled broadly. Joe exclaimed, several others dropped their forks, and the Governor of Massachusetts looked for just a moment like he might get teary. "See?" said Judy, looking around at everyone. "I have a father."

"Who is very proud of you," said George, as Judy wrapped her arms around his neck.

It took about five minutes for the laughing and sniffling around the table to stop. Judy explained that she'd had a suspicion that George was her father since she was fifteen.

"Why was that?" asked George.

"Well, for one thing, my mother voted for you when you first ran for Congress. She never voted for Republicans."

This made everyone except the Governor laugh. "I won a lot of swing voters in that election," said the Governor.

"There've been other hints over the years, but when my Justice told me I was moving back to Boston to join your staff, I was pretty sure," Judy continued. "And then there was this impulsive visit to your famous family's house."

"A family Judy is part of," Janis added.

"You'd figured it out too?" said Judy.

It seemed to Andrew that Janis hesitated for half a second before she responded. "No," she said.

Pretty soon everyone was talking at once. All the women kissed Judy, including Cynthia. All the men congratulated George. "Does anyone want more pancakes?" Joe said finally. No one did.

"Would anyone mind if I said something?" said Cynthia. "About yesterday."

"Today is better than yesterday," said Andrew.

"Today will be famous," said Judy.

Cynthia took a deep breath. "I just wanted to apologise." She looked at Joe. "To all of you," she added. "I lost my balance for a while." She paused again. "I suppose I should explain…"

"Not necessary," said George.

"We probably all have things to apologise for," said Rosemary.

Andrew realised that George was looking at his daughter.

"We'll talk," said Judy.

"So let's call it even," said Rosemary.

There was a general murmuring of agreement.

"I wondered if I could leave early," said Cynthia.

"You certainly don't have to," said Andrew.

"And I'm afraid it isn't possible," said the Governor. "The

boat that brings the papers and the milk has come and gone. There isn't another ferry until the afternoon, and that won't get you to New York before the plane I assume Andrew has booked you on this evening."

Janis spoke: "We also thought we might make some promises to each other about confidentiality."

Cynthia thought about that for a moment. "That would be good," she said. And then: "So, let's do the dishes."

That would have brought down the second-act curtain, but as everyone was beginning to get up from the table and carry their dishes to the kitchen, the front door opened and Andrew's errant wife, the primary Cathy, walked in.

12

Cathy had come on the ferry that brought the milk and Sunday papers and gotten a taxi to the house. She was wearing clothes Andrew had never seen before: a short skirt of some silver fabric that danced around as she moved, a light blue tee shirt with no bra, ballet slippers, a lot of silver bracelets. The overall effect was more feminine than anything she'd worn in years – or would have been except that she had had her hair cut so short it *just* lay down.

Cathy walked briskly around the room, introducing herself and shaking hands: "I'm Cathy. I'm Cathy. You must be Shiva."

"And you must be Ariel," said the Indian.

"Being set free," said Cathy.

"So *this* must be the end of the play," said Shiva.

It was clear to Andrew that Cathy was engaged in an enormous act of will. She had decided to be a different person. She could be charming and cheerful when the spirit moved her, but she was never this brisk and bold. And she *never* dressed to call attention to herself. What was going on?

When Cathy got to Sally she kissed her on the cheek. "How did it go?" she asked.

"All right, I think," said Sally. She introduced Cathy to Joe.

"Andrew told me I'd be impressed," said Cathy, looking the billionaire up and down as if she were flirting with him.

"It was quite a party," he said. Andrew didn't think Joe knew what to make of Cathy. But then, he didn't know what to make of women generally.

"My pleasure," said Cathy, as if she'd arranged it all.

When she got to Andrew, though, she just stood and looked at him. "I'm sorry," she said.

Rosemary had come around the table and was standing next to him. She had slipped her hand into his, which Cathy would have seen. "Eleanor was trying to reach you," he said. "You left your phone here."

"I know," said Cathy. "I bought another one. She's fine."

"You said she was having a minor crisis. But then, you said you'd gone to Germany to see her and you obviously haven't."

"I didn't say that," said Cathy.

"We need to talk," said Andrew. There were too many spectators for the talk they needed to have.

Cynthia approached, stopped a few feet away and waited for a break in the conversation – like a six-year-old on a school playground trying to make a new friend. "I'm Cynthia," she said, advancing a step.

"I know," said Cathy. "I like waking up with you. Watching you on television, that is."

"I like your outfit," said Cynthia.

"It was a mistake," said Cathy.

"But you're beautiful," said Cynthia.

"No I'm not," said Cathy. "Did Andrew tell you I was?"

"He didn't tell us anything," said Cynthia, taken aback by Cathy's tone. "He pretended Sally was you."

"You did?" said Cathy, looking at Andrew and then at Sally.

"It seemed like a good idea," said Andrew, not letting go of Rosemary's hand.

"What exactly did you say, Sally?" said Cathy.

"I told Andrew that you'd gone to see Eleanor. Not a serious crisis, but your sense of responsibility as a mother compelled you to go. That sort of thing."

"But you were supposed to tell him I'd gone away to... think about things. You were supposed to...explain."

Andrew could see that Cathy was getting embarrassed. She didn't know Rosemary, who was holding her husband's hand and watching the scene unfold. She didn't know Cynthia, even if she recognised her from television.

"Did you show him the note?" Cathy said to Sally.

"The note permitted various interpretations," said Sally. She wasn't the least bit defensive, Andrew noticed. "It seemed to me that another speed bump on your daughter's road to adulthood would throw him less off balance than confronting the truth about your sexuality. And to tell the truth, I thought it would be fun to pretend to be you. And make him pretend as well. You have a nice house. I wish it was mine."

"You thought you'd audition for the role?" said Cathy. "Since I was leaving the company, that is."

"It was a long shot, but yes."

"It didn't work, I see," said Cathy, looking down at Andrew and Rosemary's intertwined hands.

"No. But it's been an interesting weekend."

"How long did you get away with it? Did you have to sleep with him?"

"Cynthia discovered the fraud," said Sally, not answering Cathy's questions.

"I found pictures of you," said Cynthia.

"Dressed rather differently," said Rosemary.

Rosemary squeezed Andrew's hand, which he took as an instruction not to intervene.

Cathy looked around the room. "But there aren't any pictures at all," she said. "Did you throw them out, Andrew? That wasn't fair."

"Sally hid them," said Rosemary. "So she could pretend to be you."

"Well, I hope you enjoyed it," said Cathy. "The position's available. I'm not me anymore, as I expect everyone can see."

"You're the same person," said Cynthia softly. "All this" – she gestured at Cathy's clothes – "it's just wardrobe."

Andrew decided the previous evening's release of emotion must have been cathartic for Cynthia. She'd been soft and feminine all morning. She was seducing Cathy, if you came down to it. And it was working. At some level Cathy liked it, even if she didn't know how to respond and was in consequence as abrasive as ever.

"I suppose they wouldn't let you look like this on the air," said Cathy. She laughed, presumably at herself. "I'm not sure it even works in my own home – if this still is my home. Is it, Andrew? You've cleared away the photographs. Have you sold the house?"

"There hasn't been time," said Rosemary. "And you're the one who left."

Andrew felt it was unnecessary of Rosemary to intrude, but Cynthia spoke before he could. "I like the hair," she said. She spoke as if she and Cathy were alone. "Your head is a good shape," stroking Cathy's head almost unconsciously. "But no, my audience definitely isn't there yet."

"Where do you plan to sleep?" asked Rosemary. "I'll change the sheets."

"I think that's Sally's job," said Cathy curtly, not looking at the "au pair." It wasn't clear whether it was Sally or Rosemary she was trying to put down. Both of them, probably.

"I'll help you," Rosemary said to Sally.

"Maybe we can talk later," said Cynthia, still trying to soothe Cathy.

"What about?" said Cathy. She had more anger and adrenaline in her system than she could cope with, Andrew could see.

"Wardrobe if you like," said Cynthia. "I'm an actress, remember?"

"I thought you were a journalist," said Cathy.

"Not to my friends," said Cynthia. Having planted the seed, she then drifted away. Wardrobe, Andrew repeated to himself. Cathy had made Sally try on her clothes, which involved removing clothes. Cynthia intended to do the same with Cathy.

Cathy and her startling costume continued around the room. "This explains a lot," said the Governor of Massachusetts. Andrew was close enough to hear the conversation.

"You mean my refusing to let you kiss me?" said Cathy. "I was thirteen, remember."

"That and other things," said George. "I'm a politician, remember. I have instincts. Andrew is my oldest friend. Do I need to say more?"

"No," said Cathy.

"Then let me introduce you to my daughter."

Cathy looked surprised and then laughed. "Oh, George," she said.

"Thank you for having me," said Judy, looking at Cathy without embarrassment.

"Where's Lydia?" said Cathy.

"Being angry with me," said George.

"Tell her it's a lousy strategy," said Cathy. "Not that I've got a better one."

"I gave up trying to persuade her of that a long time ago," said George.

"I'm going to help wash dishes," said Judy.

"I gave up trying to be married to Andrew forty-eight hours ago," said Cathy. She must have known he could hear her, Andrew decided.

"Why did you come back?" said George. They'd known each other forever. He could ask that question.

"To talk to Andrew, I guess." She didn't look at him.

George looked around. "There are a lot of people in the way just now."

"I knew that would be the case. I was counting on Andrew's billionaires being here, to be honest, so as to make my announcement irrevocable. I guess that was the point of this stupid outfit too. I've chickened out a number of times in the past – about talking to him, that is."

"Perhaps you and Andrew should go for a walk," said the Governor. "We can manage without him for a while."

There comes a point when the string-players tire and the music slows. Having sat in silence, the horn then sounds its sad notes. Cathy closed her eyes for a moment. "All right," she said.

Andrew let go of Rosemary's hand and took a step in Cathy's direction as casually as he could.

"Lighthouse?" he asked. "Sun at our back coming home."

"I guess," she said.

They'd walked on that beach many weekends, often holding hands. They didn't hold hands this time. They didn't speak. Andrew waited for Cathy to initiate. He figured she was the one who needed to offer an explanation. He was angry, of course, if relieved. He'd absorbed a lot of rejection over the years.

"I'm angry too," she said at last, reading his mind.

"Clearly," said Andrew, more sharply than he intended.

"Not at you, sweetie, though of course I am. There's nowhere else to put the anger. But what I'm really angry at is having wasted so many years not having love."

"I loved you," he said. It was approximately true.

"It wasn't the love I wanted." She paused. "I prefer women. I'm not even bisexual. There, I've said it."

"I know. I expect I knew from early on. People generally know things and pretend they don't. Judy did that. I'll have to tell you that story. I kept busy, so neither of us would have to acknowledge our mistake."

"I kept busy too," she said. "I reckon I've done a hundred weekends worth of house guests."

"That's probably right."

"I looked at myself in the mirror one morning, soon after I'd finished nursing Florence. We were still living in Brooklyn then. We still didn't have any money but you seemed to be doing well at work. I figured you'd be a good provider for our daughters. This is the life you bought, I told myself. It was on sale. You can't return it."

"Maybe you should have," said Andrew.

They walked in silence for a while.

"I'm sorry there wasn't more sex," said Cathy.

"Not your fault," said Andrew.

More silence.

"There wasn't sex for me either," she said. "Just copulation. But that was my responsibility. Oh, sweetie, if I talk any more I'll probably just hurt you."

More silence.

"I seem to have a relationship," said Andrew cautiously, "with Rosemary. I think you met her."

"The gorgeous English woman? How amazing. Sorry, I didn't mean that as a put-down." And then: "I don't have a relationship with anyone."

"I didn't mean to gloat," said Andrew. "And yes, it is unexpected. And, yes, I have been unfaithful to you in the past two days."

"Not knowing where I was? How could you do that?"

"It just happened. If it is any comfort to you, it's never happened before." Or not completely, he added silently.

"There was that woman," said Cathy.

"The one you kissed last summer?"

"I called her once. A few weeks later. I hung up, though, when she answered the phone. That was all."

"Sally?" said Andrew, and then wished he hadn't.

"She did try to seduce you, didn't she?"

"She mostly made me nervous," said Andrew. He wanted to build some distance between himself and Sally, at least in Cathy's mind.

"I should think so," said Cathy. "Anyway, what I did with Sally is irrelevant. I'd already decided to leave. I was just trying to achieve escape velocity."

"She said you kissed."

"We did more than that."

"She didn't tell me that."

"Well, we already know she lies, don't we?"

"You realise she's a prostitute?" said Andrew. "An engaging and creative one, but still."

"That's why I hired her," said Cathy.

"You *wanted* her to seduce me?"

"It would have been an excuse for leaving you. When I hired her I didn't have a plan, though. I was just doing what you'd told me to – as I always have. Hire someone skinny and voluptuous, you said, someone to keep me company, who you could fantasise about. Go to a nanny agency, you said. Fuck that, I said. I was desperate – which called for desperate measures. I bought one of those magazines with quote personal classifieds. She was the third woman I interviewed and I thought she was perfect."

"She was," said Andrew. "She got you to let go."

Cathy didn't respond. "Tell me about what happened when you arrived and I wasn't there," she said.

Andrew recounted the events at the airport, her proposition, the fifteen seconds he'd had to decide, Sally explaining "intimacy without sex" as she undressed. He tried to make the story amusing, which was something he knew how to do. Cathy laughed. Andrew laughed. Laughing reminded them both of times they'd had fun together. They both began to cry, hugged each other, regained their composure, continued to walk.

It was still early. There was no one on the beach, though there probably would be soon.

"I don't think we'll make it to the lighthouse," said Andrew.

"We never have," said Cathy. "Except when we were herding house guests."

They turned around and walked back.

"What do you want me to tell people?" said Cathy as they

got near the house. "What are we both going to say?"

"We say we had twenty great years but our paths have separated. Those who care about either of us will accept that. We don't owe anyone an explanation. We all have failures we'd rather not elaborate on. I'm being fired Monday, by the way, or so it appears. But that's fine. I'll get over it. We have enough money." He walked on a bit. "But as to how we conduct ourselves, sometimes a bear just needs to go into its cave, wait out a winter of self-mockery and grief, and hope to emerge a better bear when the snow melts."

"I expect to be good at self-mockery," said Cathy briskly. She got impatient whenever he tried to be eloquent. "Perhaps I should be the one to talk to Eleanor," she said.

"That might be best," said Andrew. "I'll call Florence."

They were a hundred yards short of the wooden steps, the tunnel through the bushes and the house. Andrew stopped. "What are your plans?"

"I don't have any plans."

"My billionaires are leaving this afternoon, but I'd arranged to stay until tomorrow morning, to help you and Sally clean up."

"That was a nice thought, sweetie."

"The relationships have gotten a bit jumbled, though, so I don't honestly know who's doing what. Do you want to stay here?"

"Could you stand it? I'm suddenly exhausted."

"It's your house too."

Now that he and Cathy were declaring defeat, Andrew's brain was flooded with memories of roads not taken. "You go in," he said to her. "I need to walk a bit more."

Venetia of the flannel pyjamas had opened the door on

time and let Andrew in when he stood on the doorstep of her tiny house in a fashionable neighbourhood at two o'clock in the morning. She was wearing slacks and a sweater. "I was afraid you'd come," she said. They hadn't discussed it after the first night.

"Didn't you want me to?" he said.

"Of course I did. It's gratifying when men want me."

"But...?"

"I'll give you a cup of tea, or a whiskey if you want. Yes, perhaps we ought to have a drink. But then you have to leave."

He wasn't utterly surprised. She poured Glenmorangie into two glasses. They both drank it down in a single gulp.

"You aren't ready for a man who cries?" he said. He knew that wasn't it.

"I'm not ready for a man who's married and has a daughter, who lives in New York, who I am in grave danger of falling in love with."

"One kiss?"

She nodded her head to say yes.

He'd walked the twenty blocks to his hotel, letting empty taxis pass him.

When Andrew was made a partner and bought the house in Nantucket with the intention of giving his own house parties, it was called "Spouter Cottage" – a *Moby Dick* reference. He wanted to change it to "Guilty Memories," which would have been a Venetia reference, but he never actually suggested it. Cathy maintained that giving your house a name was pretentious. And to be honest, the memory of Venetia had still been painful.

It now occurred to Andrew that if he had been unfaithful to Cathy with Venetia, they might have given up on their marriage a lot sooner. Andrew would have confessed. He was that kind of man. Cathy could have said, "In that case…" and been free. So it turned out there was truth in Venetia's riddles. Cathy had been punished for what Andrew hadn't done.

<u>13</u>

By the time Andrew got back to his nameless house, the Governor had essentially taken over. Having known him since they were seventeen, Andrew recognised the signs. George became manic when there was a girl he wanted to impress. This rarely turned out to be advantageous to the girl.

Janis had been set up in the tiny study wedged among the bedrooms on the second floor. The door had been closed and all the guests had assumed it was a closet – everyone except Cynthia, that is, who seemed to have done a lot of exploring. "We need a place for Janis," George had loudly announced. "We need a place for Janis to work, to get these agreements drafted." Rosemary described the scene to Andrew when he got back from his walk with Cathy. Cynthia had suggested the study. There was a desk that faced the door, with a chair behind it and two others facing it. Andrew's Harvard diploma hung on the wall, above a small bookcase.

Seeing Janis sitting there, when he briefly looked in, it occurred to Andrew that she was good in tight places, good at making the best of things. Her humour and good manners probably didn't reflect a privileged upbringing as he had initially supposed. Her mother was probably a single parent, an underpaid, enormously competent executive secretary – same as Judy's, come to think of it – who'd taught her how to fit in, how to be indispensable, how to never make anyone important uncomfortable. And with that training and emotional endowment, Janis had found her way to the Governor's office, devoting herself to a man whose political destiny meant he could never marry her, even if he came to love her. Along with self-discipline and resilience, Janis had a talent for having her heart broken.

Janis also had a laptop. She always did. "I never know when I'll have to issue a statement," the Governor had explained, as if that would have been news. There was a printer under the desk that seemed to be willing to take instructions from the laptop. "A very helpful little machine," George called it. To go with very helpful Janis, Andrew said to himself.

George had begun by ushering people in to see Janis, one by one, and interrogating them on what they wanted or needed or felt others were entitled to. "The Grand Bargain," he initially called it. Janis took notes on a yellow legal pad. "I know how to make deals," he told Andrew when he and Cathy returned.

"Several of us know how to do that," said Andrew sharply.

Andrew was feeling far from manic. Bringing twenty years of marriage to a close didn't feel like something to celebrate, even if it was a relief. Rosemary seemed to feel that too. It was twelve years of marriage she was discarding, if he'd done the maths right. Anyway, she seemed a bit subdued.

The night before, once Sally had been outed, it had seemed to Andrew that Rosemary was assuming the role of hostess. He'd liked that. He wanted her to stay forever. Now, with Cathy in evidence, it felt like Rosemary had pulled back. Surely she didn't think Cathy would go back to being the person she'd been. Or that Andrew wanted that.

"…political deals," George was saying, warming to his subject, as six of them sat around the table drinking coffee while Janis worked away upstairs. "This is about rights and reputation as well as financial outcomes, and it's a multi-party understanding in which competing interests must be balanced."

"I have no reputation to worry about any more," said Cathy. "I'm going to my bedroom."

"So it's a 'Concert of Nantucket' you are aiming for," said Shiva, "like the 'Concert of Europe.' My uncle was a diplomat, remember," he added, as if to apologise.

The Governor liked that. "You can do the economics, Andrew," he said generously. "You'll do that better. There always have to be bankers to do the economics."

"There were bankers at Versailles and no one listened to them," said Shiva. "Keynes was there. He wrote his famous book about it."

"Keynes wasn't a banker," said Andrew. "He was an economist and a speculator."

"Versailles was a failure," said Rosemary.

"How about the Congress of Vienna?" said the Governor. "That worked, if I remember rightly."

"'Congress of Vienna' sounds like sex," said Judy. Andrew suspected everything in the world reminded Judy of sex this morning.

"Sex works," said Rosemary. "So presumably the Congress of Vienna did too."

"My wife, the optimist – who read poetry at university," said Shiva. "My soon-to-be-former wife, that is."

"Thank you, Shiva dear," said Rosemary. Just possibly, that

was his first outright indication that he intended more changes than retirement. Rosemary seemed all right with that. Andrew was more than all right that she was.

"The Congress of Vienna *did* work," said Shiva, "for ninety-nine years – from 1815 to 1914."

"So what's the difference," said Judy, "between a 'congress' and a 'concert' – diplomatically, that is?"

"A concert is a harmonious arrangement," said Shiva. "A congress is a meeting where you negotiate to achieve it. The Congress of Vienna is where the Concert of Europe was conceived, in fact. The Concert was sometimes called the 'Congress System' because there was an understanding that problems would be solved through further meetings, further congresses, rather than wars."

"Sex as a precursor to further sex," said Rosemary.

"You would have been a fine diplomat, Shiva," said the Governor, acknowledging Rosemary's contribution with a flicker of a smile. "Did you ever consider it?"

"An eldest son has no choice," said Shiva. "Not if there is a lot of money to be attended to."

"A prince and therefore a prisoner," said Andrew.

"A politician of sorts," said the Governor.

"But without the hope of losing an election," said Shiva.

"More coffee, anyone?" said George, bouncing up from the table. And then: "I'd better check on Janis."

"Leave her alone," said Rosemary.

Andrew opened his mouth to second her suggestion but then closed it without speaking. There was no point in arguing with George when he was manic. You only had two choices. You could laugh or you could get grumpy. Laughing was much the better course, but Andrew was feeling twitchy and uncertain on so many levels that his sense of humour seemed to be failing him. Don't be rude, he said to himself. Keep your thoughts to yourself. Having been told he had no immediate role, he went out onto the porch and sat on the steps.

Thinking about Venetia had been quite unsettling, actually. She'd been haunting him ever since Joe described his own experience of an English shooting party and the girl he'd failed to pursue. Venetia had visited him off and on for nineteen years.

There was Venetia getting into the bathtub, which was jolly and erotic. There was Venetia the tease, which was also erotic, and all that kissing, which felt sweet and genuine even if it was advertised as part of the teasing. Then the disappointments of his marriage had jumped out and confronted him. He'd cried like a four-year-old. And Venetia had been really nice about it, making it plain, in that oblique way the English have, that she didn't really think love was a game either, and that while she had no intention of getting involved, if he was willing to wrestle with the pain and complications of a divorce with a baby and no money, which she assumed he *wasn't*, she could be prepared to get serious. Or at least that was the shape memory gave events. "I was afraid you'd come," she'd said. And she'd been right. Whether it was cowardice or virtue, he hadn't been prepared for pain and complications. Some evenings, when he'd drunk too much, it felt like the great failure of his life. And now here was Rosemary as a second chance.

"The issues seem to be," said Rosemary quietly, sitting down next to Andrew when George went back upstairs, "and in no particular order: ensuring no one discloses the foolishness Sally got us up to last night; the fact that we all went to bed with quote, the wrong partners, unquote; your fees; the understanding

Joe and Shiva reach about combining bits of their respective businesses; Cynthia's payout from her pre-nuptial agreement; what Joe wants to offer Sally; what Shiva is prepared to offer Judy; whether Judy will accept anything – so far she refuses; who gets the seats on this evening's flight to Manhattan, and if Cynthia isn't one of them, who fills in for her on breakfast television; what story George tells Lydia – he hasn't brought that up but it's hovering over us like the *Hindenburg*; whether any of us need to vouch for him; whether we should; whether we have enough left-overs; whether Cathy will spend the night here or is going to ask Lydia for a bed; whether whatever Janis, poor girl, drafts would stand up in court if anyone wished to contest it; what court would have jurisdiction – oh, and I nearly forgot, how does Shiva go about giving Joe sufficient authority over the rest of his multi-billion-dollar empire to persuade Joe to take charge of it, which Shiva continues to want to do even though Janis tells him he shouldn't." She paused. "That's my list, anyway."

"What about you?" said Andrew. There was just a little space between them on the step, he noticed.

"I spend tonight in the servant's room with you no matter what. I assume that's not negotiable."

"I suppose we have to make lunch," said Andrew. No, it certainly wasn't negotiable. Maybe he should have said that.

"And dinner for whoever's left," said Rosemary.

"Should we go to the store?"

"In a bit. You should probably talk to George some more. He's too excited to be thinking clearly. In fact, the people who should go to the store are Cynthia Jane and Rosemary." Andrew raised an eyebrow, which Rosemary ignored. "You should talk to Joe and Shiva – separately. They both seem to trust you."

"Why do you say that?"

"They told George they do."

"That's nice." It was more than that. For an investment banker trying to be "broker to the deal," it was the ultimate accolade. But Andrew wasn't opening any champagne yet. There was a lot of anxiety in the air.

"It's a sort of hybrid agreement," said Joe when Andrew found him in the garden.

Andrew was only half listening. I should have told Rosemary I trust her, he kept saying to himself. She's *my* broker. She's my *salvation*. I must tell her the next chance I get. "Yes, Joe," he said aloud, having missed Joe's last sentence.

There were a couple of surprisingly comfortable cast iron chairs in a corner of the garden. Joe had been sitting in one of them, by himself. He'd looked from a distance like he was meditating but that seemed unlikely. Andrew didn't think Joe was a meditating kind of guy.

"Shiva and I can bind ourselves as individuals," Joe repeated. "We can promise you your fees. You've 'performed.' I told Janis to put in a 'whereas' to the effect that you've brought us together and enabled us to see the path we plan to go down and that your work is essentially done. But neither of us can bind our companies. I have shareholders. He does too, at some levels of the organisation chart, but there's also his family. All we can do here in Nantucket regarding the deal itself is sign a loose agreement in principle. But we as individuals can agree to pay you the $40 million if our companies don't."

"It ought to be $20 million," said Andrew. You'll never succeed as an investment banker if you give money away, he told himself.

"I know. Scale would be $10 million each. And you'll

never succeed as an investment banker if you keep giving money away."

"Rosemary was probably confused when she said twenty million each. Anyway, it was never my money."

"I doubt very much that Rosemary is ever confused," said Joe. "But I do like it that you raised the matter with me. I'm happy to leave it at $20 million each if Shiva agrees. Janis is drafting it that way. I'll talk to Shiva about it."

"That's very kind of you," said Andrew.

"Well, look, there's some other stuff you've done that I probably can't pay you for, so it's fine."

Even on Wall Street, Andrew told himself, getting a finder's fee for reconnecting a client with a friendly dominatrix was probably unusual. "Are you...?"

"Yeah," said Joe. "I've talked to Cyn. The divorce process will start next week, which has settled her down a lot. We've both known it wasn't working. That's part of what made her come unglued last night. I've just got to figure out where to put her for the next couple of months. She can't stay in Greenwich. Sally will be there."

"Cynthia commutes from Greenwich?" Andrew said. "She would have to leave the house at five in the morning to get to the studio."

"She does – or did. But she liked the whole Greenwich concept. She liked being there on the weekends."

"So you could barbeque," said Andrew.

"Cyn says living in Greenwich allows her to be normal. She says television is an artificial world."

If Greenwich meant normality, Andrew wasn't sure about Sally living there.

"If you have a car pick you up at five," said Joe, "it's

surprisingly quick getting into the city. I've ridden in with her a few times to see how it worked. She didn't like having me in the car. Cyn has to read the newspapers every morning, of course, and she does that then. Part of her shtick is knowing what's happening in Europe. If she needs an update from network people in London or Paris or wherever, they can do that while she's in the car too. And I suppose the trip in from Greenwich is when she puts on her game face.

"But I do have to find her a place to live in Manhattan – like maybe tonight."

"I could let her stay at my apartment. I'm not going back tonight."

"What about Cathy?"

"I can't answer for her. I asked her what her plans are and she said she didn't have any. But she's here tonight, I think. I'll ask her about Cynthia staying in the apartment, at least for a few days."

"Only if it's easy," said Joe. "I can put her in the Four Seasons. That would attract curiosity, though, Cyn being a celebrity."

"Leave it to me," said Andrew.

"Right," said Joe. "But what you need to apply your excellent mind to is how Shiva puts me in charge – in charge of his whole empire, that is – and whether in the end he wants that. It sounded simple this morning on the beach, but it would be a pretty extraordinary thing to do and it will take the better part of a year to do the due diligence and have all the shareholder votes and family pow-wows that will be required.

"What I do not want, meanwhile, is to ignore the control issue for the deal that brought us to Nantucket on the theory that that will just happen naturally as part of the larger deal, and then to discover the bigger deal isn't going to happen and we haven't addressed the governance issue for the smaller deal. The larger deal isn't a merger, after all. It's a management agreement – I think. Or a treaty of friendship if we're honest about it. Your deal *is* a merger, albeit at a subsidiary level. And I want to make sure *it* happens."

"I see what you mean," said Andrew. He hadn't, to be truthful, taken in this wrinkle. Shiva offering to put Joe in charge of everything could be a way of backing Joe into a corner where he did the smaller deal without an adequate shareholders' agreement. Just because they'd all been naked didn't mean Shiva hadn't had something up his sleeve.

He stood up, thinking about George's statement that Shiva would have been a good diplomat – a gentleman sent to lie abroad for the good of his country, as Henry Wotton famously put it in the seventeenth century.

"Wait," said Joe. Andrew sat down again. "The deals will sort themselves out," said Joe. "Or if they won't, they won't. But what do you think of the personal stuff?"

"Sally?" said Andrew.

"Right."

"Well, now you know why you thought you'd met her before."

"Wasn't that an amazing coincidence?" said Joe. "I'm just not sure about living with her in Greenwich. Or, to be precise, about *her* living in Greenwich. It's practically the capital of the hedge fund industry, as you know, so there are a lot of very aggressive personalities living in those houses on five-acre lots and trying to join the yacht club. Some of them will have met her before – in one capacity or another."

Joe didn't say any more. "She still *amuses* you?" Andrew

asked him. "I think that was your word."

"Typical British understatement," said Joe with a smile. "I'm being facetious, of course. But I definitely want to hang onto her. She's like hundred-proof whiskey when you're fourteen years old. Or being James Bond and having your balls wired up to the generator."

"Not my idea of fun," said Andrew.

"Probably not a good analogy, but I think you get my point. She's more than amusing. Oh, and by the way, congratulations on winning last night. I don't often get beaten at anything…"

"But you like being beaten," said Andrew.

Joe got a quizzical look on his face for a moment and then smiled. "I see what you mean. Yes. Fuck. I do. Or I do in a certain way and up to a point – which Sally seems to be able to find. Having a wife who can light you up is very useful for a person in my position. I'm too – what word do I want? – too established to go to prostitutes anymore."

"You don't mind that she once was a prostitute?"

"Personally? Not at all. They're the only honest people in the world, I sometimes think."

"Others are not so broad-minded," said Andrew.

"My point exactly," said Joe. "And I worry about Sally being snubbed. If she marries me, she's going to encounter some of that."

"If she so much as goes out to dinner with you, the gossip magazines will get to work and uncover her whole history."

"Oh, I don't mind the gossip writers, and she probably doesn't either. That's just back story. It's the interpersonal stuff, and what happens now. Like, here's a scenario. I give a million dollars to some charity, which I often do, and there's a big fund-raising dinner. The wife of a million-dollar donor ought to be on the committee for the dinner, go to lunches, make new friends. But the worthy matron who's organising it calls me up and says maybe Sally shouldn't be on the committee, because there are some religious assholes on it who might make Sally feel awkward. Make the worthy matron feel awkward is more like it. Anyway, that would hurt. Sal would pretend she didn't care, but it would hurt."

"Can I make an irregular suggestion?" said Andrew, but Joe kept on speaking.

"And here's what it really comes down to, Andrew – since I believe in facing reality. I'm not sure I could make it *not* hurt her. I've been married three times already and I haven't been able to make one of them happy. I don't want to keep marrying perfectly nice women and making them unhappy, even if I make them rich. I told you I don't get beaten very often, but to be honest, marriage has defeated me."

"Could I make an irregular suggestion?" Andrew repeated.

"And that's what I've been sitting out here brooding on," Joe continued. "Hell, I probably trust Shiva. I want the little deal buttoned up, but you and I both know how to do that. Sorry, what is it you keep trying to say?"

"You should talk to Rosemary," said Andrew.

"Really? Why?"

"She knows a lot about gossip and convention and... maybe you and Sally should live in London. It works better from a time-zone perspective. It's a more sophisticated city. Not a lot of born-again Christians in Belgravia. Probably not a lot of Sally's former clients either."

Joe laughed. "Interesting idea. Spanking's higher status there too, if the jokes mean anything."

"That was probably an earlier generation," said Andrew.

"Well, anyway, the Brits certainly aren't as hung up about sex. Why is that, Andrew?"

"The Puritans came *here*."

Joe laughed again.

Andrew went back into the house and looked for Shiva. He was in the study with Janis and George. "I know we came to this magical island to do a simple deal," the Indian was saying, "where we combined a couple of businesses that cried out to be merged, but now that Judy has suggested it, I admit I am very attracted by the prospect of having Joe manage everything. I want that to be part of what we agree to today. Once my lawyers get a hold of me, I'll never be able to do it."

"That's exactly why I can't let you commit to it," said Janis. "It wouldn't be ethical. You have to have your own lawyers."

"Well, I'm happy to put in the document that you advised me to that effect and I declined to take your advice."

Janis looked dubious.

"That would work legally, I think," said Andrew.

"The issue for Janis is how it looks – how it looks to people who will never see the 'whereases'." George might or might not have known how to do deals, but he understood about appearances. "This whole transaction, if it happens, will get a lot of scrutiny. Janis's role *could* get a lot of scrutiny. She has to be squeaky clean – and be seen to be so."

"Thank you, Governor," said Janis.

There's love in her voice again, Andrew told himself. Love and sadness. She's seen George get manic before – about all sorts of things. She's seen him cool off. She assumes he will make up with Lydia, as he always has done, and that it will be awkward to have Janis continue on his staff. She assumes the document she's drafting will be the last thing they work on together. "Goodbye, Janis" will be an unspoken "whereas."

"But we won't solve this problem by worrying about me," Janis continued. "How committed can Joe and Shiva be without actually being committed?"

"They can announce an intention," said Andrew. "And if they don't follow through they could be accused of market manipulation."

"The Stock Exchange gets very testy about that," said Shiva.

"And they could hold a joint press conference to explain what they have in mind," said the Governor. "It would trash their reputations if they didn't follow through. That's how politicians bind themselves. They go on television and make themselves hostage to thirty seconds of footage."

"So what we should be drafting," said Andrew, "isn't an agreement in principle but a press release."

"I need to introduce my family and business partners to the idea gradually," said Shiva.

"Why don't you tell us again," said the Governor, "what you had in mind when you said you wanted to put Joe in charge?"

"Can Judy listen?" said Shiva. It occurred to Andrew that he was asking George's permission.

George seemed to take it that way too, and pondered the question for a moment. "Sure," he said finally. "Janis?"

She got up from the desk and went in search of her intense young friend.

"The thing is," George said to Shiva and Andrew as soon as the three of them were alone, "I think I should keep Janis out of this – not on television, not identified as having drafted this document."

"Not here at all this weekend, George?" said Andrew.

"Umm," said the Governor.

"Joe and I will want to pay her for her assistance," said Shiva. "We can't give Andrew $40 million and give Janis a bottle of wine."

"We need to talk about that number," said Andrew. "It should be twenty."

"Joe told me you'd say that," said Shiva. "I told him it was up to him. See, I'm trying to let him make the decisions."

"We can see that you are," said George. "But going back to what we were talking about, I admit I personally don't want to get any publicity about being here with Janis – and certainly not about Judy – but I don't think they would want it either."

"Fair enough," said Andrew. He thought for a moment. "How about this? Shiva, you and Joe can't announce the big deal because you can't promise it will happen. No one would believe you if you said it was any kind of certainty. But you can sign a memorandum of understanding about the smaller deal, as you call it, with appropriate provision for getting whatever board and shareholder approval is required. It is arguably a material transaction for Joe's group so there needs to be an announcement. The announcement includes a final paragraph that says the two of you are *also* exploring further cooperation. You can leave that pretty vague. The market will assume it's just make-nice bullshit. You might say you will need to do a market-by-market anti-trust analysis, because you will."

"Of course you will," said the Governor. "Which is why no assurance can be given of anything coming of this broader cooperation."

"Could you put Joe in charge of the task force looking at that?" said Andrew. "That would allow him to poke into anything and everything. He'd talk to you about any decisions that he thought should be made. You'd see how you felt about taking his recommendations, which would be the first step down the road of giving him authority."

"He'd see how he felt too," said the Governor. "About checking with you at all."

"Joe poking into dark corners of my empire would be fine," said Shiva. "They could use some sunlight. And we've seen each other naked, so to speak. But he's going to have to do it without bringing a lot of his lawyers in. From what I hear, his lawyers are pretty aggressive, which in parts of my world could be taken as disrespectful. Not that they shouldn't be thorough. It's a style thing, mostly." He paused. "I'm a prince, remember?"

"How about if we get Joe to hire Janis's firm?" said the Governor. "She has a light touch."

"That she does," said Andrew, "but..."

"And if she needed to get word to you on something," the Governor said to Shiva, "she could call Judy."

"Janis doesn't work for a firm," said Andrew.

"She's going to," said the Governor.

"Which one?" said Andrew.

"I'm not sure yet," said the Governor.

At this point, Janis and Judy reappeared. The little study was crowded. Shiva tried to give Judy his seat, but she made him stay put and slid behind the desk to stand next to Janis's chair.

"Shouldn't we have Joe here?" said Shiva.

"Not yet," said the Governor.

"So what's the question again?" said Janis.

Judy looked at Shiva. An indecipherable message passed between them. Or perhaps she was just telling him that in the hour they'd been apart she hadn't lost interest in him. Men can always use reassurance. "From what Janis has told me," she said to George and Andrew, "you are puzzling over the question of how Shiva gives Joe authority over his *unmerged* businesses. This is not actually a problem for Shiva but for Joe. Joe is a decisive individual. He will find it difficult to not have complete authority. He also has a reputation as a manager to protect. And independent directors. Even though he controls the majority of the vote, he, and those directors, have a duty of care to the other shareholders – which by the way includes care for his own reputation, which is worth a couple of p/e multiples. Isn't that right, Andrew?"

Andrew nodded.

"Joe knows he cannot go wandering off helping Shiva run his empire," Judy continued, "unless his market cap is protected and there is an upside for his shareholders. I suspect that's what he's sitting out there in the garden thinking about. I suspect Joe would like to just do the deal Andrew brought them and see how that works out."

"I thought you were supposed to be unworldly," said Andrew.

"Well, it's obvious," said Judy.

"I want to do the bigger deal as well," said Shiva softly. "I want Joe's help immediately. Now that the idea of having his help has presented itself, I am desperate for it. I know I should not confess that, but you are all trying to advise me, so I must be truthful. If I have to go back to India and argue with my brothers one more time I will get physically sick."

Andrew decided he believed him – decided *to* believe him. There was still doubt floating around in his brain. The reputation for temper tantrums – though maybe that was just a reflection of his being exhausted. The subordinate who'd saved him $50 million who he wouldn't give a bonus to – though that could easily be an urban myth. Rosemary's over-the-top statement that he needed to regard Joe as a vassal probably was true at some level. But the Indian did genuinely seem to be out of gas.

"So, you need to let this be Joe's deal," said Judy.

"He needs to be Lord Castlereagh," said Shiva.

Janis looked puzzled.

"Key player at the Congress of Vienna," said the Governor.

"I'll fill you in," said Andrew.

"Shiva is going to take a nap," said Judy. "Tomorrow we are going to fly to India so I can see a tiger."

"And meet my family," said Shiva.

"Only if they behave themselves," said Judy.

"So, Janis," said Shiva, pulling himself together, "this treaty you are ghostwriting. We've given it a name, which George can explain."

"I'll fill you in," Andrew repeated.

"It needs to provide for Rosemary," said Shiva. "Joe says she has to get whatever Cynthia gets. Talk to Joe about that. The more you talk to Joe the better. But as for the rest, for the next couple of hours, Judy has my proxy." He stood up to go.

"I'll be back in a minute," said Judy.

"You don't suppose he's having a heart attack, do you?" said George when the two of them had left.

"God, I hope not," said Andrew. That was all he needed. He was about to make a joke about Judy keeping Shiva up all night making love, but he remembered that the Governor was Judy's father. And, of course, he himself had spent the night with Shiva's "soon-to-be-former" wife. Everyone seemed to be accepting the pairings made the previous evening, but it might be better for the deal if they kept sex in the background. If that was possible.

"I think where we are," said Janis, "is that over the next few months, Shiva will be giving Joe access to his companies and his people. Joe can't do Andrew's deal without a certain amount of due diligence, and I suspect Shiva's empire isn't compartmentalised the way an American corporation would be. There's no knowing what's connected to what. Joe will have to turn over a lot of rocks. If in the process he finds a decision that needs making, he'll tell Shiva. If Shiva demonstrates – to Joe and to himself – that he is able to just do what Joe suggests without a lot of fuss, well, that's the real due diligence they need to do for the bigger deal. Right?"

"Nicely put," said Andrew.

"And we put something in the announcement about 'further cooperation,'" said the Governor.

"Which Shiva can point to," said Andrew, "if any of his brothers or vassals think Joe's due diligence is getting too extensive."

"You understand how this works?" said the Governor to Janis. "Shiva is the one who wants the bigger deal, but he tells everyone Joe's the one who wants it, and he's humouring Joe in order to get the smaller deal done, which is what he, Shiva, wants – when in fact Joe's the one who cares about the smaller deal. See?"

"Yes, Governor, I see," said Janis softly.

Just for a moment they were looking at each other as if they were alone, as if Andrew wasn't in the room. Andrew couldn't help wondering when George was going to tell her which Boston firm she was joining. But maybe they had more of an understanding than Andrew knew about.

Judy came back into the study.

"How is he?" said Andrew.

"Asleep already," said Judy. "Now you boys go amuse yourselves – and talk to Joe. In fact, send him up here so I can understand what he's doing for Cynthia. Then I suggest you let Janis and me go to work."

"And the confidentiality bit?" said the Governor.

"Of course," said Judy.

Minutes later Andrew was summoned back upstairs. "You need to resign," said Janis.

"So I won't be fired?" said Andrew.

"Being fired would be better than resigning," said Judy, "from a financial point of view, that is. I assume you have some unvested stock options they can take away from you if you quit. But you can't sign fee agreements with Joe and Shiva until you *have* quit."

"In fact," said Janis, "and speaking hypothetically, it would be better for you to quit out of anger and without knowing what you're going to do next."

"Do you know how to get angry, Andrew?" Judy asked.

"Of course I do," said Andrew, suddenly feeling that his masculinity had been questioned. He tried to suppress that thought, however. Bankers who feel their masculinity is being questioned tend to make mistakes.

"Do you have your relevant colleague's number?" said Janis.

"My 'technical' boss?" said Andrew, remembering Joe's comments about facing reality. "I regret to say I kept his number on my mobile phone. Force of habit."

"Call him now," said Janis. With the Governor out of the room, she could be quite commanding. "You've heard they've moved your office without telling you – that would be a good place to start." He'd forgotten he'd told Janis about that. He'd needed to tell someone.

"He may not even be up yet," said Andrew. "The client outing can go pretty late. I mean, I want to do it with a bit of class. I don't want to be an asshole."

"So much the better if you wake him up," said Judy. His mobile was in his pocket but he hesitated, so she went on. "Fish it out. And don't hold back. We want to *watch* you be an asshole."

"We *advise* you to be an asshole," said Janis with a smile.

Andrew told Rosemary all about it. "I'm unemployed," he said. "I feel terrific." He and the two young lawyers had come downstairs for a celebratory glass of orange juice.

"He was rude and reckless," said Judy. "We advised him to think twice."

"I have a fair amount saved that I can live on," said Andrew.

"I pointed out he could live another fifty years," said Janis.

"He may never get another job on Wall Street," said Judy. "Not after what he called the man who used to be his boss."

"His 'technical boss,'" said Janis.

"Perhaps you can get a job in a bookshop," said Rosemary. "Or a diner."

"Perhaps I should work on my sandwich-making technique," said Andrew.

"I think you'd better," said Rosemary. The two young lawyers went back upstairs. Andrew and Rosemary went into the kitchen.

"Before we start making lunch…" said Andrew.

"Yes?" said Rosemary.

Before he could answer, Sally came in. "You need to tell

me if I should pack," she said.

"I would think so," said Andrew.

"Well, I saw you talking to Joe in the garden. He hasn't exactly told me what's happening. There aren't enough plane tickets to get everyone back to Manhattan. Some of us have to spend the night. Someone has to drive your car back, Andrew, whenever you go..."

This would have been the right moment for Andrew to indicate that he planned to stay on Nantucket for a while, and that he hoped Rosemary would stay with him, but there was a loud knock at the front door, which he thought he should answer.

It was Lydia, looking for George.

"I'll see if I can find him," said Andrew, glad that Janis was tucked away in the upstairs study. It seemed to him that Lydia was overdressed for Nantucket. She always was.

"I just need him for a minute," said Lydia. "I'll wait on the porch if you want."

"Don't be ridiculous," said Andrew. "Come into the living room."

Lydia sat on the front half of the sofa. She was clutching a small paper bag.

"Can I get you anything?" said Rosemary.

"No thank you," said Lydia. "Oh, here he is."

"Would you like us to leave you two alone?" said Andrew.

"No need," said Lydia. "Sit down, George. It will all be public soon enough."

Andrew held his breath. George looked resigned.

"I have a confession to make," said Lydia, "and a request."

"I want to help with lunch," said Cathy, coming down the stairs. It was in the nature of an announcement, Andrew observed. She wasn't speaking to anyone in particular.

"Oh, hello, Lydia," said Cathy.

"What have you done to your hair?" said Lydia.

"It's a long story," said Cathy. "But will you stay for lunch?"

It was Cathy's house, Andrew reminded himself. And yes, it was a long story. And probably not one to tell Lydia.

"Thank you," said Lydia. "I will not. George, here's the… item I found in the washing machine." She handed him the paper bag. "And here's my engagement ring." She pulled it off her finger and handed it to him. "And my wedding ring."

George said nothing. Andrew assumed he'd been through this sort of thing before.

"I've met someone in California," said Lydia. "He lives in Pasadena." This sounded like a new departure.

"Your mother's not actually dying?" said George.

"Of course not," said Lydia, as if the idea of her seventy-something mother expiring was absurd. "I keep coming back to talk to you, and then you do something to make me angry, so I postpone it. But I can't wait any longer. I want a divorce. I want to marry Harold."

"And live in Pasadena," said George.

"Yes," said Lydia.

George thought about that for a moment. "You never wanted to leave California in the first place, did you?" said George.

"And I shouldn't have," said Lydia.

Having delivered her message, Lydia stood up. "You can come back to the house after five tomorrow," she said to George. "I have movers coming in the morning to pack up my things. You can keep the furniture. It belongs to the house. And the house belongs to American history, as you like to tell people. And even if it didn't I wouldn't want it. I've never liked Nantucket."

Goodbye Lydia, Andrew said to himself. He'd thought she was a mistake from the day he met her. Odd that George should have proposed to her when he could have married anyone he wanted.

"How would you like to do this?" said George.

"Oh, you can tell people I left you for Harold. I *have* been sleeping with him." She said it a bit primly but with obvious pride, looking around the room to check reactions. "That way, you're the injured party. You can still be President."

14

Lydia closed the door behind her. For several seconds everyone just looked at each other.

"George," said Rosemary briskly. "Come with me."

"What?" said the Governor, who was still presumably in shock.

"I need to go to the store. You can drive me. Your car is blocking Andrew's." This wasn't true, actually.

"I'm in the middle of a deal, Rosemary," said the Governor. "I thought you were going to go with Cynthia."

"I think she went for a walk. But *everyone* is in the middle of a deal, George. What you need to do now is get out of the way. Isn't that right?" she asked, looking around for confirmation.

"Probably," said Janis, who seemed to be transfixed half-way down the stairs. She would have heard the end of Lydia's speech.

George walked over to the stairs and handed her the paper bag Lydia had given him that contained the black lace underwear. It seemed to Andrew that George should have smiled as he did that, but he didn't.

"Maybe you *should* take a breather, Governor," said

Andrew. "I'll come with you."

The three of them went to George's car. The Governor drove. Rosemary sat beside him. Andrew got in the back seat – and seemingly became invisible.

"I had to get you away from there," said Rosemary, as soon as they were on the road and heading into town. "I need to speak to you in your capacity as a parent."

"Are you a parent, Rosemary?" said the Governor.

"No," she said, "but I feel like one. I feel responsibility for that sweet young woman you have brought into the world."

"I've felt responsibility since before she was born," said the Governor. "I've paid a lot of bills – anonymously, of course."

"Well, now you can get directly involved," said Rosemary. "So tell me this: do you really think she should run off with my husband?"

The Governor gave her three answers: "I thought you didn't want him anymore." And then: "Anyway, she's an adult. It's up to her what she does. We don't even know each other. What I think should be of no consequence." And after a further moment of reflection: "Probably not."

Rosemary responded that she hadn't *discarded* Shiva – oh, please, but you have, Andrew said to himself – that George shouldn't think of it that way and that Shiva was an excellent person. Regarding George's second set of comments, she observed that while Judy might be a certifiable genius she had the emotional maturity of a twelve-year-old, and that having wished for a father all her life, and now having one, she would care what that father thought even if he turned out to have the acuity of a goldfish, which was not the case with George. Rosemary thought there should be a cooling-off period on the Shiva business, as the law required for certain major purchases by innocent consumers.

But I don't want a cooling-off period, Andrew said silently. And by the way, Judy is wiser than she looks.

"So you want to go back to New York with Shiva this evening?" said the Governor.

"Not necessarily," said Rosemary. "I might want to stay here tonight. I might want to have another chat with your daughter. I doubt her mother told her much about men. I know a bit about men – especially Shiva. And by the way, you might want to talk to Shiva."

"You think he should ask for my blessing?" said the Governor. He made a joke of it, but the thought was there.

Rosemary didn't answer. "And then there's Janis," she said.

"I have to get her off the island," said the Governor. "If you and Judy both stay here tonight, there will be a seat for her on the plane to New York. I assume Andrew's billionaires have commitments – and Cynthia has to be on television early tomorrow morning. If Janis can go to New York this evening, she can catch the last shuttle to Boston from there and be in her office early tomorrow and not arouse anyone's curiosity."

"I assume Sally who isn't Cathy will be taking the fourth seat," said Rosemary.

"What's real Cathy – damn it, I've known her for thirty years – what's *Cathy* going to do?"

"Andrew hasn't told me."

It seemed very odd of Rosemary to speak of him as if he weren't there. If she was sending Andrew a message, he didn't like it.

"Well, they can't very well stay together now that she's come out," said George. "Dramatic, the way she did it, showing up with her hair cut off."

"You and Lydia have stayed together for a pretty long time," said Rosemary, "despite your different natures."

"At least we're both heterosexual," said George, "as Lydia was at pains to point out. Some people have suggested I am excessively heterosexual, in fact." He seemed to be *annoyed* at Cathy for being a lesbian.

Rosemary waited for George to finish parking at the shop before she spoke again. "So why did Lydia put up with you?" she said.

"I assume she found me attractive – at least at the start. Some women do. Not my fault. Maybe she wanted to live in the White House some day. How should I know what goes on in women's heads?"

Neither of them seemed inclined to get out of the car yet. Andrew held his breath.

"Maybe she loved you," said Rosemary. "If someone loves you, you *should* know what's going on in their heads. Or at least you should try."

Again Andrew wondered if Rosemary was speaking to him, though she continued to pretend he wasn't there. But how was he supposed to know she was worried about Judy – or what Rosemary thought about Janis, for that matter? She'd encouraged Judy to sleep with Shiva in the first place. They were both nice girls, and he didn't want either of them to get hurt, but they weren't Rosemary's concern, he would have thought. They hadn't been up to now. What was Rosemary up to?

"Well, I can't do much about what I'm like at this point," said George. "But what am I supposed to do about Judy?"

"You *are* concerned, aren't you? You just didn't want to admit it, even to yourself. Typical male behaviour."

It occurred to Andrew that Rosemary was making it all up. She wasn't a conventional woman, and certainly not one who complained about stereotypical male behaviour. She was a goddess, and goddesses didn't complain about men. They turned them into frogs or struck them dead.

"So what would you have me do about Judy?" said George.

"Take an interest. Examine the situation. Talk to Shiva. Talk to her. There's clearly a powerful infatuation. What do your instincts tell you about the longer term?"

"My instincts all have to do with politics."

"Meaning dreams and weaknesses," said Rosemary.

The Governor stopped talking and stared at Rosemary for a long moment – not something many people could make George do. "My profession in a phrase," he said. "My whole life, actually. I wish I'd met you when I was in college."

George had always had a fund of pick-up lines.

"Then I would have met Andrew sooner," she said – which was nice. "But I would have been eight," she added.

"True," said the Governor. "But go on about dreams. I like them better than weaknesses."

"Dreams compress reality," said Rosemary, "same as poems do. If you think about it, dreams are poems and poems are dreams: alternate manifestations of the same essence. That makes you a poet, George."

"Now you sound like Shiva."

"No, I sound like me. He learned how to do it from me, if the truth be known. He read engineering at Oxford."

"Andrew talks that way too, sometimes," said George. "Or he used to in college. He did very well at Harvard, you know. Sort of a waste, his ending up on Wall Street. But his family didn't have any money, so he thought he ought to make some.

Which he has. Which is commendable."

Fuck you, George, Andrew said to himself.

"It is easier to imagine him as a professor than as a Wall Street titan," said Rosemary. She paused. "Except for the courage."

What was that supposed to mean?

The way they had now both embraced the convention of acting as though he wasn't there suggested there was something they were trying to tell him. Or Rosemary was trying to tell him.

Or maybe she was just filling space with sound. She hadn't expected him to come to the store at all, so she had to be improvising. She'd had a plan to have a private conversation, which Andrew had frustrated. So now they were playing an impromptu game of talking about Andrew and pretending he wasn't there. They were teasing him.

Andrew was playing along because...well, perhaps the best explanation is that he did so automatically. In twenty years as an investment banker he had trained himself to shut up and listen when a chief executive started to talk, to hear especially the messages the speaker wasn't conscious of sending. Not everyone in his profession had acquired that skill, which was remarkable. If you could learn what the man across from you thought or wanted, you could tailor your pitch accordingly and improve your chances of being hired.

Sitting there in silence, the message Andrew thought he heard being inadvertently conveyed by his companions was that their understanding with each other was superior to anything Andrew might think he had with Rosemary. George and Rosemary had sex appeal beyond what an ordinary mortal like Andrew could offer or withstand. The Governor quote had to get Janis off the island unquote, so he and

Rosemary could have Olympian sex.

Pretending to care about Judy was a *clever* improvisation. It was a natural subject for Rosemary to raise with the girl's father. And it was something that would be awkward to talk about in proximity to either Judy or Shiva, so it was a plausible reason for her to have wanted to be alone with George. But she couldn't really care about Judy.

"You believe in dreams," said Rosemary. "Joe believes in reality. Shiva believes in his own divinity…"

"And Andrew?"

"He's been through a lot in the past few days," said Rosemary. "He may not know where his head is. But if he does, I wish he'd tell me."

"Andrew believes in work," said the Governor. "Always has."

"Worse than that," said Rosemary. "He believes in virtue."

"But look," said George, having nearly exhausted his capacity for thinking about anyone else's problems. "It is quite unlikely I can deter Judy from going to India. She's a very determined person. You should have seen her in the study."

"I have no intention of going into that study," said Rosemary. "What happens there is men's business, even if your daughter and her friend choose to involve themselves.

"What you must do about your daughter," Rosemary continued, "is to show concern. If she's unhappy a year from now, she'll like it that you paid attention. She'll talk to you. Look at poor Andrew. He doesn't seem to have paid sufficient attention to his daughters and now one of them hates him."

"I thought that was supposed to be a phase," said George.

"One other suggestion," said Rosemary, abandoning the matter of Eleanor, "and then I'm done. Ask Janis's advice." The

Governor didn't respond. Rosemary offered no explanation. "You stay here," said Rosemary, opening the car door.

Maybe he and George were supposed to talk. George must have thought so because he kept clearing his throat.

"You realise what's going on here?" George asked him.

"Probably not," said Andrew.

"She's feeling guilty about leaving her husband."

"But her husband is having an affair with Judy – which she herself encouraged."

"Maybe I should have said she's feeling *nervous* about leaving Shiva. She'll go back to New York with him," said George. "You watch. And she's persuading herself that she's doing it out of concern for Judy."

Andrew didn't like what George was saying, but George had always known more about women than he did. Or at least he went out with prettier girls. Frighteningly beautiful girls, in fact. Like Rosemary. Andrew didn't really believe George and Rosemary were plotting to jump into bed together, but *something* was going on.

They sat in silence. Andrew was reminded of the scene in *The Godfather*, where a thug in the back seat strangles the thug in the front seat with a piano wire. A hand grenade of anger exploded in Andrew's brain. "You know a lot about women, don't you George?"

"No. I've just slept with a lot of them."

"But you think Rosemary is going back to Shiva?"

"I do, but it doesn't prove anything that I think that. And Andrew, I should have said this long ago: do not envy me my quote success with women. It is as much a burden as a blessing. I have never had a successful relationship that lasted more than a few months, and I don't expect I ever will. Once I possess a woman, her fascination has a half-life. But these lovely girls keep presenting themselves, and when one does it makes me irrationally hopeful."

"You get manic."

"You think I don't know that? You think I don't feel stupid every time?

"You know, I married Lydia because she *didn't* fascinate me. I'd finally learned how to work hard – in law school – and I said to myself, what I needed, as a future politician, was not a dream marriage but a *workmanlike* marriage. That was the word I used. Be like those clever Indians. Marry someone *suitable* and don't ask for too much. My marriage to Lydia was an arranged marriage, only I arranged it myself."

"It didn't work."

"Obviously. I'm stupid about love even when I am not in love."

More silence. Finally, Andrew asked the question he had been avoiding: "Are you planning to sleep with Rosemary?"

"Of course not," said George. "I never plan anything. Sex is something that happens to me. But Andrew, in thirty years of friendship, have I ever stolen a girl from you?"

"No."

Rosemary got into the car and George drove the three of them back in silence. Andrew had had a dream, the previous night, he now remembered. In parts of the dream he knew he was dreaming and in parts he thought he was awake. Like most dreams, it was confusing, though no doubt there was insight to be extracted from it, provided you had the energy. The fact that something made no sense didn't prove it wasn't valid. Dreams are a category of reality.

One of the ways Andrew had succeeded on Wall Street

– this was clear in the dream but also true – was by not taking himself too seriously. This was one of the reasons his technical boss so pissed him off. The man pretended. First of all he pretended to be smart and in charge and important. The fact that he was all these things only made it worse. Second, he pretended to know what was going on – or as black Americans in the movies sometimes put it, what was going down. Which he didn't. The reason Andrew hadn't grown up with a house on the Jersey shore, only an understanding that they could rent the same one every July, was that his father worked for the government, which of course didn't pay much. And about the only satisfactory thing about his relationship with his closed-up father was that when he was sixteen he had realised that his father did something secret and important, and he'd never asked his father any questions, and his father had appreciated it. If your father's an intelligence officer, not asking questions is a way of showing him respect.

When it occurred to Andrew, in his dream, that something of a spy nature was going down, he could only laugh at himself for thinking that. He was a middle-aged investment banker. His father had been dead for ten years. There could not be shadows in his garden.

But there were. Andrew knew a lot about shadows. Shadows in the market were what made deals possible.

In the dream, he'd been asleep, and had been awakened by an absence of sound. One of the reasons he knew he was not making up the threat was that when he whispered in Rosemary's ear that there were unexplained people in the house she put her hand on his mouth, very gently.

"Do you have a knife?" he'd asked her.

"I'm not Rosemary," said Janis. "Remember?"

"Sorry," he'd said.

She didn't go on about his forgetting who he was in bed with, which was just another example of her excellence. It would not have been a good moment for a lot of arm-waving. Also, he didn't think he'd spoken either name.

"There's a wine glass," said Janis, "if that's helpful."

"Umm," said Andrew.

Improvise a weapon, Andrew's father had told him, in a rare unguarded moment. So he got out of bed, delicately broke off pieces of the rim of the glass, and went into the hall, where some people he didn't know had just finished dealing with an individual who probably wasn't a Unitarian.

Perhaps the lesson of the dream was that you just had to deal with things. "Wine glass," said someone whose face he never saw. "Good thinking."

Andrew went back into the bedroom he seemed to be sharing with Janis and let her hold him until he stopped shaking. "Who were they after?" she said finally. "And well done, by the way."

"Shiva, I suppose," he said. "I think there was only one of them."

"There is never only one," said Janis. "And George is also an obvious target."

They lay in each other's arms for a bit. It had not previously occurred to Andrew that she was the Governor's protection detail. This did raise a question though: why had she let Andrew go into the hall? Perhaps to help him maintain the edge Wall Street required.

"Do I need to do anything else?" said Andrew.

"Given that you're still alive, no."

When he woke up, it took Andrew a minute to remember

that none of what he thought he remembered had happened. It was a dream. Dreams were poems, according to Rosemary. When they pulled up at his house, he forgot his dream for the second time.

George said he needed to talk to Janis and went up to the study. Presumably he intended to consult her about Judy, as Rosemary had "suggested." Rosemary said she needed to find "Cynthia Jane." She told Andrew he was in charge of lunch and walked away. Another command. Sally said she'd help but Andrew ignored her offer and immersed himself in hamburger cookery, which he was actually pretty good at.

Shiva materialised in the kitchen. He'd been lying on his bed, wide awake, not having died but having slept for no more than twenty minutes. "Where's Judy?" he asked.

"Out in the garden, talking to Joe," said Sally. She continued to hang around.

"And Cathy?" said Shiva.

"Back in her room," said Sally.

"I suppose at some stage you'll be wanting to get your clothes," said Andrew. Knowing she was a prostitute made him want to be polite to her, but he feared it kept sounding like he was telling her to leave.

"Mostly I've been wearing Cathy's," she said. "My own things are in the servant's room – so let me know when it would be convenient for me to go in there.

"But no hurry," she added. "I assume I'll be here until tomorrow or Tuesday. There will be a lot of clean-up. It won't be hard to get a mid-week plane ticket, will it Andrew? Or if you and Cathy are flying to New York, I could drive your car to the ferry and take it back there for you later."

Andrew found this speech remarkable. Joe was sitting in

a far corner of the garden, trying to figure out how to make Sally both rich and happy, while Sally reassumed the role of domestic servant. And like a good domestic servant, she was ignoring the fact that Cathy and Andrew were in the process of separating. She was ignoring everything that had happened in the past two days, if you thought about it. "Maybe you should set the table," he told her.

Minutes passed. Andrew made a tossed salad, made hamburger patties, thought about his daughters. One was angry and one was not. Florence had always been accommodating, even when she was three years old. If you told the two of them, "Change of plans. We're not going to the circus today after all," Florence would look up at you like an angel and say, "Next week?" Eleanor would turn bright red and break a lamp.

In a corner of his consciousness, he saw Sally go out onto the porch, stare at the ocean for a while, sit down in one of the wicker chairs. The thought floated past that she was probably exhausted from the burden of pretending to be Cathy, and now that Cathy had returned, from the burden of pretending everything was fine. Was he supposed to do something about that – and if so, what?

On Friday, Sally had had control of him. "Suffering instructs," she had blithely told him, and it was clear who would be doing the suffering. Now he had control of her. She was a supplicant, asking to be given a chore to do so she wouldn't feel awkward. "Control" was a word, and a concept, that sometimes had erotic content, but just now it didn't seem to. Just now it had to do with the accidents that control our lives. Andrew had married Cathy because he thought he ought to, even though abortions could be legally obtained. Cathy had seemed to be keen on the idea. Neither of them had had a clue about the other – and they chose to regard their foolishness as romantic.

Cathy had turned out to have both of their daughters' temperaments at once. She went along, and then was angry that she had, which produced in Andrew an endless cycle of hope and disappointment. Shiva was right – was it Shiva or someone else? – right that we have several natures, which "manifest" at different times. He might have added that we have alternative fates, which take control at different times. Andrew didn't know much about Indian philosophy. Perhaps he should look into it. It occurred to him in a languorous way that perhaps everyone at the house party was part of one collective consciousness. This was succeeded by the less peaceful thought that in a collective consciousness, everyone would share everyone else's happiness but also everyone else's pain.

15

As if to demonstrate this proposition, everything then happened at once.

George reappeared. "I need to talk to you," he said. "Can't someone else worry about the hamburgers?"

"They'll be ready in a couple of minutes," said Andrew.

"No one but you will be ready for lunch in a couple of minutes," said George.

"What am I supposed to do, then – take them off the grill half cooked and finish them later? That works with steak but not with hamburgers." He might have added that George's co-conspirator Rosemary had insisted he start making lunch, but just then Rosemary came in.

"You realise that young woman is sitting on the porch weeping?" she said.

"Sally?" said Andrew.

"Of course," said Rosemary.

"I need to talk to you, old friend," said the Governor in that famously persuasive voice he had. He wasn't interested in Sally's problems.

Cathy burst into the kitchen. "Andrew," she said without

preliminaries, "Florence is engaged. She just called. I said you'd call her back right away." She was radiant.

"His name is Richard, right?" said Andrew.

"Of course it is, you silly man," said Cathy. She was ten years younger.

Rosemary turned away and went outside again. She wouldn't have liked that flashback to a happy marriage.

"I'd better call," said Andrew. He handed the Governor the hamburger turner.

"I left my phone in our bedroom," said Cathy. "Just hit 'recent calls.'" *Our* bedroom.

"I am not a hamburger chef," said George to the retreating Andrew.

As he went up the stairs, he thought he heard Cathy saying, "Be a good sport, George," which would have made him laugh if he hadn't been so full of uncertainty. No one had ever gotten George to do anything.

At the top of the stairs he heard quiet sobbing. It was coming from the tiny study. He could hear it through the door. His good angel told him he couldn't ignore it. Janis – he assumed it was Janis – was in the tiny study in service of the deal, in service of his fees. She was in Nantucket serving the Governor. Whatever had just passed between them had made George need to talk to Andrew. Florence was presumably happy. She could wait five minutes. He opened the study door.

Janis looked up. "I'll be all right in a bit," she said. "I do apologise. No, come in. It's your house." She wiped her eyes. Andrew closed the door. He sat down across the desk from her. "The Concert of Nantucket has hit a speed bump," she said, attempting a laugh.

"Go on," said Andrew.

"I guess I thought I would be part of the deal," she said, "after Lydia's dramatic appearance."

"Do you want a hug?" said Andrew impulsively. He probably knew what she was going to tell him.

"Yes, but I'm not entitled to one," said Janis. She'd almost recovered her competent professional tone. "Let me explain."

"Not required," said Andrew. He felt foolish having offered to hug her, but she didn't seem to hold it against him.

"If I tell you what happened, I can put it behind me. And you're easier to talk to than anyone else." She gathered herself together. "I mistakenly assumed, based on Lydia's professed readiness to let the Governor divorce her – rather than the other way round – that what happened last night could be the start of something. The Governor and I would gradually 'come out' as…good friends. At the appropriate moment, we would become more than that. Publicly, that is. Sounds silly when I say it, but girls have dreams.

"I was startled when he and Rosemary went to the store the minute Lydia left. He should have wanted to talk to me."

"You and George did sleep together last night, right?" said Andrew, remembering his dream.

"As did you and Lady Rosemary," said Janis.

"Doesn't sex trump talking?"

"Yes and no," said Janis.

Andrew knew it was absurd to let doubts about Rosemary creep into his own brain.

"I knew it was absurd to worry about the Governor going off with Rosemary," said Janis. "And I am very good at not worrying about things I can't do anything about. So I sat up here drafting."

"You didn't share your worries with Judy?"

"Of course not," said Janis. "She was glowing with happiness. I sent her to quiz Joe about pre-nups. But then the Governor reappeared and began explaining why Judy shouldn't go away with Shiva. Like he was Judy's father or something."

"Which he is."

"Her technical father," she said with a smile. "Her biological father. But he hasn't paid much attention to her up to now. I mean, she's happy about it, but I have to say it was pretty slack not make some sort of contact in all those years."

"He paid her tuition."

"She got scholarships."

"They were made to look like scholarships," said Andrew.

"That's illegal. He would have gotten a tax deduction for a charitable contribution to Harvard when what he was really doing was spending his money on something he wanted. I don't honestly think either the Governor or Harvard would have done that."

"Neither of us has seen his tax returns..."

"They aren't the point," said Janis. She paused and smiled at him. "And you and I don't need to be arguing. The point, as it affects *me*, is that I don't think he was talking about Judy and Shiva. He was talking about George and Janis. Judy is too young, he said. Shiva is too old. He isn't that well, even if he looks healthy. He could leave her a widow in only a few years. Shiva has a position in the world that would expose Judy to 'uncomfortable journalistic attentions.' That was his phrase. Judy has her whole life ahead of her. Marrying Shiva would shut off too many possibilities." Janis slowed. "That sort of thing. No thought being given to Judy's feelings, actually." She paused again. "It came to me that he was breaking the news slowly."

"No more four-poster bed," said Andrew.

"Oh, I might sleep with him tonight." She laughed. "It would be a way of kissing my dream goodbye."

"Well, I wouldn't make any assumptions," said Andrew. "He suddenly had an urgent need to speak to me. It's hard to know what's going on in his head."

"The Governor is a world-class politician," said Janis. "You never really get to see what he thinks."

"But he has to know you're in love with him," he said.

"What difference would that make?" she said. "Hundreds of women think they're in love with him."

"They don't work in his office," said Andrew. "They haven't devoted every waking hour to him for – what is it? – three years. Have you even had a date with someone else in all that time?"

"Umm," said Janis.

"I'll take that for a 'no.'"

"Close enough," she said. They sat in silence for a moment. "You know, the thing is," Janis continued, "I'm probably not in love with him, or not in the way adults ought to be. I took the job because it seemed exciting, and then I became intoxicated with the situation. I became the heroine of my own invented love story – something my mother distinctly warned me about."

"Because she'd done the same?" said Andrew.

"Good guess," said Janis. "So I suppose the real reason I was crying was out of embarrassment."

Andrew wanted to ask a question but he hesitated. "Did you start to cry before he came downstairs?"

"Of course not," she said.

There was a knock at the study door. The Governor stuck his head in. "It's OK," he said. "I don't need to talk to you after all, Andrew." He looked at Janis. "I talked to Shiva. He

211

understands. And lunch may be ready." He stepped back into the hall and closed the door.

"You see?" said Janis, who now seemed to be in complete control of herself. "This is not about Judy. But I've got to prevent him from messing things up for her."

"You think she should actually marry an Indian prince who is older than her father?" said Andrew.

"Quite possibly," said Janis. "She's good with grown-ups. She entered Harvard when she was fifteen. If she thinks it will work, it will probably work." She paused. "And she doesn't have to marry him tomorrow. At least she ought to get to see a tiger."

Andrew started to have a thought about how admirable Janis was, pushing her own disappointment aside to worry about her friend, but he suddenly remembered he was supposed to be calling Florence.

"Come down to lunch as soon as you feel up to it," said Andrew. "We can talk some more if you want this afternoon – or we can put this whole conversation down the memory hole if that's easier for you – but right now I have to make a phone call."

As he went to find Cathy's phone, it occurred to Andrew that maybe he should have kissed Janis. On the cheek, you understand. As a way of expressing sympathy. For a moment he imagined kissing her. The desk would have been in the way. Andrew hoped Janis wasn't going to haunt him like Venetia. She'd been in one of his dreams already.

What Cathy had failed to tell him was that she had told their daughter they were separating, providing an explanation that, if indirect, was easy enough for a young woman living in San Francisco to decode. After ten minutes of waiting for his phone call, Florence had turned into Eleanor. She was mightily upset. "Daddy, what have you done to Mom?" she said.

"Pretended she loved me," he said.

"What a shitty thing to say," said Florence, who rarely used that sort of language, even if her sister and her parents did. "What a shitty thing to do. You should have let her go years ago, if what you're both telling me is true. And by the way, I do not want wedding pictures with my parents' gay lovers in them."

"I'm not gay," said Andrew.

"How come you could live with Mom, then – she being what you secretly knew she was?"

"I found her attractive. We had some good times. I can be slow to figure things out." Andrew considered but rejected the idea of telling Florence about the many ways reality could manifest. Or about "house rules." Nor did he attempt to persuade her that he *hadn't* known. He needed to keep things simple.

"Well, just stay together for eleven more months. Richard and I plan to get married when he graduates. We want to have the ceremony in Nantucket."

"I hope you don't plan to drop out of college," said Andrew.

"I know. Mom would kill me – or it would kill her. But I'll definitely finish. I'll transfer my credits. I'll figure out how to do that once we know where Richard will be working, which will probably be San Francisco. We don't want children for ten years. I want to establish my practice first."

Andrew should have gone downstairs right away but he needed a minute. This was Cathy's bedroom. His too, but his wife made the rules. Memories swelled up the way the sea did when there was a storm offshore. "Never trust a woman," he remembered Cathy saying to him once. He'd been outfoxed by one at work, when he was an associate, and his wife had scolded him for it. "Women are natural liars," Cathy had told him. "We make nice because we have to." Even then, Cathy had been trying to confess.

The girl in question had flirted with him, which was impossible not to enjoy, and he'd forgotten to defend his turf. She'd wound up getting credit for a deal that should have been his.

Who was his unhappy wife warning him about now – or his subconscious warning him by calling up memories? It occurred to him that he hadn't figured Judy out. According to Janis, she was brilliant. According to Rosemary, she was soft. What she had to do with Andrew he could not imagine. But she was her father's daughter, so you didn't get to know what was going on in her head.

The Governor had been a *leitmotif* in Andrew's life since the first week of college. Andrew was rather proud of having George as a friend. If George's daughter became Mrs Shiva as a result of this house party, Andrew would like that too.

Meanwhile, did he need to fear the next Mrs Shiva? He did not. If there was a problem, Janis would take care of it.

"They want to get married next June," he announced to the lunch table when he came downstairs. "Here in our garden." And love has made my daughter daft, he didn't add. She cannot imagine anything ever going wrong.

"That would be lovely for you," said Rosemary, presumably referring to a Nantucket wedding, though for a moment he thought she meant never imagining things going wrong. There was a politeness in her tone that troubled Andrew, but there was too much happening for him to brood about it.

"Where's Janis?" said Joe, having come in from the garden.

"She'll be down in a minute, I expect," said Andrew.

"She wanted to finish something."

"We need to talk about logistics," said Joe cheerfully. Shiva was right about the man. The prospect of managing something – anything – made him happy. "I understand we only have four tickets on the plane back to New York. I have meetings first thing Monday morning, so I'm afraid I need one of them. Cynthia needs to be there too, as we all know. Her audience expects it. Shiva?"

"I have a little more flexibility than you two. Rosemary, you have a luncheon date, if I remember."

"I can get there via Boston," said Rosemary. "That is, if one of the Governor's advisers is prepared to stay the night here and lets me have her ticket to Boston. I assume you have to fly back this afternoon, George, so I'll go with you. I can take a shuttle from Boston to New York." She left the table and went outside before anyone could agree or disagree.

"I'd quite like to go tonight," said Cathy.

"So that would be Shiva, Cathy, Cyn and me on the plane?" said Joe. "You'll have to pretend to be Rosemary, Cathy."

"They let me change the names on the tickets," said Andrew.

"How are we on the drafting, Janis?" said the Governor. She was just sitting down at the table. "You know, they shouldn't let you do that, Andrew," he added. "Cathy could be a terrorist."

"I can be done in about three hours if Judy helps me," said Janis. "And assuming I've understood what everyone wants."

"We all probably need to spend a couple of hours being sure of that," said Shiva. "I can stay in New York until Wednesday."

"But I can't leave Massachusetts," said the Governor. "Perhaps we could get the confidentiality matter done today though."

215

Andrew could see his deal disappearing like a sandcastle at high tide.

"You're speaking at some learned society's annual dinner on Wednesday night in London, Shiva dear," said Rosemary, who had come back inside but continued not to look at Andrew. "And you are very tired. The fact that you couldn't take a proper nap today just proves it. You need to fly back to London on Monday morning on your own plane and have two nights in your own bed before you're expected to stand up in public and explain the coming surprises of the twenty-first century. I think that was your topic. I'll make my own way back on a commercial flight and be there to hear you." She paused. "And before you sell all the seats on tonight's puddle-jumper, remember that there is a young woman on the porch who is probably entitled to a ticket."

"I assumed Sally would be needed here," said Joe. "For a day or two." Astonishing that he contemplated leaving her on Nantucket. What was it Judy had said about the very rich regarding everyone else as servants?

"I can stay if that's required," said Sally, who had pulled herself together and had just come in. She was obviously speaking to Joe, but he didn't seem to know that. She looks destroyed, Andrew said to himself. Disappointed expectations could do that. "And no, I won't have any lunch," Sally continued. "But I wouldn't mind lying down, if someone could tell me what bedroom to use."

"I'm out of the servant's room," said Rosemary.

"Thank you," said Sally, and started in that direction.

Andrew needed to talk to Rosemary, who seemed to be angry at him. He needed to talk to Joe, who seemed to be his only remaining client. He needed to talk to Cathy about staying together for eleven months, though he didn't see how they could do that. He was unemployed. He could use a lie-down himself, but that wasn't feasible. He didn't have a bedroom any more.

"Cynthia," said Joe. His wife had appeared at the kitchen door. "I've saved you a seat on tonight's plane, but where have you been?"

"I was hiding out in the maid's room, but the maid required it."

"The Maid Required It," said Shiva with a chuckle. "That could be another one of your movie titles, Rosemary." No one laughed. It seemed to Andrew that a month had passed since that first dinner.

"What do you mean, 'hiding out?'" said Cathy.

"It's a long story," said Cynthia.

"Oh really?" said Cathy, holding Cynthia's gaze. Cathy was still wearing the dramatic costume she had arrived in – and no doubt feeling uncomfortable in it. Cynthia had re-cocooned herself in fame and glamour. Cathy thought Cynthia was ridiculing her, and was becoming hostile. That sort of thing happened with Cathy.

Andrew caught Rosemary's eye. "We need to talk," he said.

"Not yet," she said.

Janis caught the Governor's eye. "We need to talk," she said.

"I think you need to be drafting," he said. "Which we all really appreciate." He looked around the table. "Could everyone please acknowledge that Janis is doing us all a big favour?"

Murmurs of agreement.

"Ask Judy to join me when she can," said Janis. She folded

her napkin as if to leave the table but remained seated. She looked exhausted.

"Where is she, anyway?" said Shiva.

"She's in the garden, I think," said the Governor.

"Why is Judy still in the garden?" said Rosemary. "Didn't anyone tell her lunch was ready?" She too looked worn out.

"It's sort of a pick-up lunch," said Andrew. He felt it must be his fault Judy hadn't been told. Something was clearly his fault, anyway.

"We need to know what she wants to do tonight," said Joe, still absorbed by the cannibals-and-Christians problem. "That is, we need to know eventually, so everyone gets on the right plane – or the right ferry.

"Oh, and I'm not forgetting about you, Sally," he added, looking around "But where is she."

"Thank you for your concern," said Judy, coming in with a plate of food. "Sally's lying down," she said. "In answer to your question, Rosemary, I was aware that lunch had been served. But I had some thinking to do." Soft sweet Judy had evidently been listening from the kitchen – and was the only one of them who hadn't lost her nerve.

"I've been doing some thinking too," said the Governor, "and we need to talk."

"No we don't, father," she replied.

"I've had a conversation with Shiva," said George.

"With respect, father, you didn't have a conversation. You made a speech."

"You talked, didn't you, Shiva?" said the Governor.

"Not as such," said Judy.

"I listened," said Shiva. "And then I talked to Judy."

"So now," said Judy, "would you all please listen to me?

And Cynthia, would you ask the maid, as you call her, to come back?"

There was some moving of chairs and fragmentary conversation as Sally was retrieved. "This feels like the end of a detective story," said Joe.

"No corpse yet," said Rosemary.

"*I* am going to see a tiger," said Judy. "My strategy, which I recommend to anybody who needs one, is not to be afraid." She looked at Rosemary as she said this. "Shiva and I will be on the plane to New York tonight, and to London tomorrow. I will see to it that he gets enough sleep. I will listen with interest to his views on the surprises of the twenty-first century, one of which is clearly me."

"Don't drink the water," said Rosemary. She was washing her hands of Judy.

"Joe will also be on the puddle-jumper," Judy continued. "He needs to be in New York when the press release goes out tomorrow morning. The Concert of Nantucket will come into being in the next three hours, and *parts of it* will have to be disclosed.

"The fourth ticket should go to Sally. She has finished her work here."

"But Cyn has to be in New York before dawn," said Joe.

"No, I don't," said Cynthia. "I've called in sick."

"You have?" said Cathy, suddenly brightening. "I didn't know you were allowed to do that."

"I've given myself permission," said Cynthia. "A person has to do that sometimes," she added softly. "Anyway, the woman who fills in for me when I take vacation will be delighted."

"We need to go back to work, Janis," said Judy.

"Yes, we do," said Janis cheerfully. She had pulled herself

together well. She believed in work. The two young lawyers left the table.

The Governor started to stand up as well, but Shiva put a hand on his arm. "I appreciate your concern for Judy, George," he said, "but I'll look after her. And it would be really helpful if you didn't apologise to Janis until the document is finished."

"What am I supposed to apologise for?" said the Governor.

"Being yourself," said Shiva.

"What's happening, please?" said Joe, who had lost his grip on the logistics.

"There have been some misunderstandings," said Andrew. "But it's being sorted out. You can apologise to Sally whenever you want."

Joe looked over at Sally. "Wasn't I clear?" he said. "You're coming to live with me. I just didn't think we'd want to leave Andrew with all the laundry and dishes."

"I think you failed to mention that," said Rosemary. "And you're a billionaire. Hire cleaners."

"Oh, I intend to do that, but someone has to supervise them, which I thought Sally could do since she knows the house."

"Joe, you're an idiot," said Cynthia, smiling. "Not that I'm not one too from time to time," she added.

"It's all right, Cynthia," said Sally. "I'm a prostitute, remember. I know all about being used." She dropped her voice an octave. "But I may have to punish him for it." Her billionaire blushed.

Rosemary walked around the table and put her hand on Andrew's shoulder. "If you can tell me which bedroom is free," she said, "I might just take a nap myself."

"Use my room," said the Governor. "I'm not sleepy."

Rosemary went upstairs without a word. Joe suggested to Sally that they put her things in the room they'd shared the previous night. Cynthia announced rather quietly that she and Cathy were going for a walk. "Topless?" Andrew was tempted to ask but didn't. Everyone was naked enough already.

Andrew was left at the table with Shiva and George. "Just out of curiosity," he said, "what was it you urgently needed to speak to me about, and then didn't after you spoke to Shiva?"

It took a moment for George to register the question. "I was trying to figure out how to get Janis to Boston tonight, but after Shiva told me he wouldn't take Judy with him, I realised there would be room for Janis on the plane to New York tonight, which solved everything."

"But now," said Shiva, "Judy has claimed that seat."

"And claimed you," said Andrew,

"So it would appear," said Shiva.

"And there isn't room for Janis after all," said Andrew.

"Nor a need for Rosemary to get to New York," said Shiva. "She doesn't really have a lunch, by the way. I was just giving her an excuse if she needed one. I'm well trained. And I'm glad she's taking a nap," he continued. "She's no fun at all when she's tired. So what are you going to do, George?"

"I guess I'll stay here," said the Governor. "Our tickets to Boston are actually for the morning plane. Maybe I should just let Janis get a good night's sleep, and to hell with what people think when she gets to work at noon."

"Isn't that what you always intended?" said Shiva.

"Judy was going to be coming in then too, which would have altered appearances."

"Sorry to be absconding with your alibi," said Shiva.

"And she's my daughter too, remember. But it's all right."

221

The Governor paused and looked at Andrew. "Maybe I do need a nap."

"I can recommend the servant's room," said Andrew. "I think it's empty now."

George stood up and started in that direction. "Servant of the people," he said over his shoulder.

16

The best improvisations end where they began. Andrew set the table for dinner. They were six again, though three were new. Rosemary said it was a "Left-Overs Feast." It wasn't clear whether she was referring to the food or the people eating it.

Andrew put Rosemary next to himself, and Janis next to the Governor. It was Cathy's house as much as Andrew's, as he kept reminding himself, so she had to be at the opposite end of the table, with the Governor on her right. This put Cynthia between Rosemary and Cathy. Andrew thought that could be awkward for Rosemary, given the tension there had been between the two St. Elizabeth's alumnae all weekend, but Rosemary said it was perfect.

"We talked," Rosemary explained. "In the maid's room, where she was 'hiding out,' as she put it. I told her she'd been very brave at school, that I admired her for that, and that I'd never realised she had a crush on me. 'Schoolgirls have them,' she said."

"She isn't facing reality yet?" said Andrew.

"No. I was wrong," said Rosemary. "She knows what she is. She's just always been very discreet about it."

"So she married Joe for the money?"

"Yes and no. I expect she's been telling herself she's bisexual, that all she needed to change gears was a sufficiently masculine man, and that Joe was the answer."

"And she's behaved oddly all weekend because she doesn't know what gear she's in?"

"Correct," said Rosemary, "though if I could refine your metaphor, I think she's been out of gear and free-wheeling downhill for the past forty-eight hours. This weekend has been pretty scary for her. The great thing about her television job is that it puts her in a bubble."

"Joe told me she didn't like having him ride into New York with her. He said that's when she puts on her game face."

"Joe had it backwards," said Rosemary. "That's when she could take it off – because the game she was playing was with Joe."

"So what's she up to with Cathy? That was strange when they met this morning." Andrew continued to feel protective of Cathy, he realised.

"Cynthia is fascinated by Cathy's narrative, if I can use that term," said Rosemary. "Cathy has come out – awkwardly but unambiguously. Cynthia admires Cathy for that. She's jealous. She's wondering whether Cathy can teach her how to be that brave. And Cathy wasn't being much help because she needed all the emotional energy she had just to get through the morning."

"You think they can be friends? Lotta hostility this morning, as Joe would put it."

"They went for a long walk, so perhaps. But it's not our problem," said Rosemary. "Definitely not yours, at least."

"Not yours either, I wouldn't think," said Andrew. "Why

do you want to get involved? To be blunt about it, what do you have to contribute to the situation?"

"I guess I owe Cynthia from being a shit at school," said Rosemary. "And in answer to your unfriendly question – what can I *contribute*? – I can be rude. Which can move things along. And which you do not have a talent for, sweet Andrew. But I'd better look after the cheese."

Rosemary was a genius of sorts, and like most such persons, she could be prickly. Don't tell me I'm beautiful, she'd said. Tell me I'm wise. She knew she was beautiful. Those were the cards she'd been dealt. What she had to be saying was that she wasn't sure about the wisdom joker. She couldn't seem to find it in her hand. She was using tough-mindedness as a substitute.

Cynthia came downstairs for dinner wearing the dress Sally had worn to the airport Friday. "Cathy's clothes fit me," she announced proudly.

"Amazing," said Andrew quietly.

"I find most of life amazing," Rosemary said.

All in all, Andrew was feeling pretty good. The "Concert of Nantucket" was essentially complete. They'd signed a document, at least, which committed the ten of them to take further actions – negotiation of details in good faith, et cetera – and not to disclose the weekend's adventures. Janis said it was an agreement in principle but not a contract. "It will only work if you want it to work," she said.

"Which we do," said Shiva.

Then everyone had hugged everyone else and Andrew drove the four ticket-holders to the airport.

Andrew was now forty million dollars richer – pre-tax, that is. It made him giddy to think about it as he drove back to the house. Even allowing for the division of assets his separation from Cathy would involve, he had more than enough to live on. And he was now employed by Joe, which would presumably mean further deals to concoct and opportunities to increase his net worth.

Cynthia would be a very rich woman quite soon – as would Rosemary. Judy had continued to reject the idea of a pre-nuptial agreement. "I am not afraid," she repeated.

"But you should be," her father had said.

"What for?" she had said.

Joe had stepped in and solved the problem by writing her a personal check for a million dollars. "This will get you home if Shiva turns into Caliban."

"Do you really have that much money in your checking account?" said Sally.

"It comes in handy," said Joe.

The Governor, whose nap hadn't lasted half an hour, had a lot of difficulty not being in charge. Andrew took pleasure in observing this. He reminded his old friend that his only concern was the confidentiality matter – "that and finding Janis a job at a good law firm."

"Oh, right," George had said.

"So Joe can hire her."

"Right."

"And she can be less…visible."

"Right."

"Why don't you take Rosemary for a walk or something?" Andrew had eventually suggested in the late afternoon. Janis had said it would be quite helpful if someone got the Governor out of the house. "We're getting into the home stretch," said Andrew. "I have to check the economics, as you put it. Rosemary has had a very fine nap, she tells me, and now needs exercise.

226

It's late enough that she won't burn. If we let her into the kitchen, she'll break more glasses." He said this with Rosemary standing there, paying both of them back for the game they'd played in the car.

Rosemary was charmingly silent about when or whether she would ever leave. We'll tidy that up later, Andrew said to himself. Not everything in life needs to be spelled out. He'd taken the course in international politics his junior year. He knew about the Concert of Europe. It mostly wasn't written down.

When he'd returned from the airport, and Janis was almost ready to announce dinner, Cathy came downstairs, dressed in another of her summer dresses, but a different woman. He was getting used to her short hair. She was smiling. She handed Andrew her mobile phone. "Go out on the porch," she said. "It's Eleanor."

"Hello?" he said to the mobile uncertainly.

"Thank God," said his elder daughter, who had evidently exchanged temperaments with Florence.

"Yes?" said Andrew. "That is to say, indeed."

"I couldn't stand it, Daddy. You were both so unhappy and you wouldn't face up to it. I couldn't say anything. A daughter can't. That made me angry. I'm sorry."

"I wonder if you could speak to your sister."

"I already have. I told her if she plans to get married, she has to grow up. She's still set on June, but beyond that..."

"And how are *you*, Eleanor?"

"Gleefully heterosexual, if that's your question. Nice German boys all over the place. Being fucked in a foreign language is extremely sexy."

Andrew didn't say anything. He was her father.

"That was your question, wasn't it?" said Eleanor. "I'm glad you asked. Facing reality is good."

"That's what my new boss says."

"Oh, yeah, Mom said you have a new job. You've quit the firm and now work for a billionaire. Is he a nice billionaire?"

"He's taken."

Eleanor laughed. "Mom said you have a new partner too – a gorgeous Englishwoman, who's a lot younger than you."

"Is younger OK?"

"Sure. Just so you're happy, Daddy. But listen, some people are waiting for me downstairs. We'll talk again soon. I've missed you."

Andrew had to spend a little while on the porch composing himself before he could go inside. It was nice Eleanor didn't hate him anymore.

The first person he encountered was Janis. "Are you all right?" she said. "Cathy said that was your daughter."

"I'm fine," said Andrew. "How about you?"

"Exhausted."

"I should think so. You did a great job. Did Joe or Shiva by any chance mention paying you?"

"Joe took my bank details. So I guess something will show up in my Christmas stocking."

Dinner was cold steak, warm baked potatoes, green salad, the last bit of the extraordinary Gorgonzola cheese Rosemary had brought in the box with the dark red ribbons, plus ice cream and raspberries for dessert. Rosemary told them all to put the Gorgonzola on their potatoes, which at least some of them tried. Andrew opened a couple of bottles of Barolo, and even Cynthia had some. They could certainly have been excused for drinking too much, but no one did. We're fragile tonight and we know it, Andrew told himself.

Cathy insisted that Andrew and Rosemary tell the story of arriving at the airport and finding Sally there instead of her. "George and Janis deserve to hear it – and I want to hear it again."

"Well, I had no idea at first," said Rosemary. "I was busy being surprised to encounter you again, Cynthia Jane."

"Who figured it out first?" asked Cynthia. "I know I was last."

"Joe," said Andrew. "He'd done some research on Cathy and me before he accepted our invitation. He'd seen pictures of Cathy."

"That's outrageous," said Cathy.

"He is a clever man," said Cynthia. "The problem is that he's a man." Everyone laughed.

At some stage, Andrew realised that Cathy – and therefore his daughters – would never hear about the game Sally had made them play on Saturday night. It had been air-brushed out of history, which was fine.

"So what was the point of the note?" said Rosemary.

"Sally was supposed to tell Andrew I'd finally acknowledged that I'm... well, that I'm a lesbian, and that I'd gone back to Boston, which is where I come from, to think about what to do next. I spent the weekend in a hotel," she said, "walking in the Public Garden and visiting familiar places. I had this theory that returning to my roots would make things clearer, but what I was actually doing was giving Andrew time to absorb what Sally was supposed to have told you." She looked down the table at Andrew. "I couldn't face telling you directly," she said.

"Important things are often difficult to say," said Cynthia. This was hardly a profound observation, but it seemed to turn her into a serious person. For the first time all weekend, Andrew decided, the idea that Cynthia was an award-winning journalist *wasn't* preposterous.

There was some passing of the cheese board and filling of wine glasses, as they all reflected on her statement. "Speaking of difficult…" said Rosemary.

"Yes," said Andrew.

"I'm not going to sleep with you tonight, brave Andrew. I'm going to sleep with George. I don't want to spend the rest of my life wondering what that might have been like."

"Does George know this yet?" said Andrew, looking at his old friend, who was attempting to pretend he wasn't listening. Andrew wasn't entirely surprised by Rosemary's announcement. He was relieved, actually.

"George is finding out approximately now," said Rosemary. "He's known a lot of women, though, so he may have seen it coming. I may have hinted at it when we went for that walk you sent us on."

"You did kiss me," said the Governor.

Part of Andrew expected Janis to get up and leave the room, but she didn't, which was interesting.

"George's wife left him today," Rosemary went on, "and my husband is taking his new young friend to India, so neither of us need to feel guilty about being unfaithful. I am looking forward to finding out what not feeling guilty is like. I've been unfaithful to Shiva for years, and I've always thought poorly of myself for it." She paused but no one spoke. "You're a fine man, Andrew. Shiva's turning into a fine man too. Some days I almost forget he's a prince. Having thought about it – and yes, Cathy, it can take a bit of time to come to terms with things – I realised that what I need is a man who's as selfish as I am."

George just smiled at her.

"As to you and Cathy, Cynthia Jane, congratulations on your courage. It makes you both beautiful in your summer dresses." She paused. "*More* beautiful, that is." Another pause.

"Which leaves Andrew and Janis. We haven't talked all weekend, Janis. I won't make a long speech now. I suspect you two are quite compatible – which is not as common among couples as one might suppose. So I recommend you just go upstairs and slip into bed."

Andrew thought he ought to say something, but Janis reached over and put her hand across his mouth, so he didn't. "May we be excused?" she said.

"I'll do the dishes," said Cathy.

And did they all live happily ever after? It's too soon to say, but the signs are good. Divorces that need to happen are in process. Weddings are being planned. The "small" deal has closed and the bigger one looks increasingly feasible. Joe has turned over a lot of rocks and hasn't found as many centipedes in Shiva's empire as he expected. Shiva lets him deal with what he finds.

Judy got to see several tigers, made friends with Shiva's adolescent children, charmed his mother, terrified his half-brothers, made her husband-to-be get plenty of sleep, sent Janis lots of postcards. Shiva has bought a historic house on Beacon Hill, on the theory that when Judy has mastered the "real world," she will teach at Harvard Law School. He hasn't told Harvard that yet, but presumably her father will, at the appropriate time and in the appropriate way. George has explained to Shiva that the right time to endow a chair of Hindu Studies is *after* Judy gets appointed. Meanwhile, she has taken a job at a proper Boston firm, in order to apprehend *that* version of reality. Her employers are astonished by her erudition. Shiva is astonished by her capacity for work. She continues to be astonished by sex.

Cynthia helped Cathy with the dishes and wore one of her tee shirts to bed. They moved into Cathy and Andrew's New York apartment for a while, but decided they wanted something that was unequivocally "theirs" – in Greenwich Village rather than Greenwich, Connecticut. They do sometimes take out their fear and anger on each other, but they always make up before they fall asleep. Cynthia hasn't cut her hair, and they've kept their relationship out of the magazines, but her off-duty wardrobe has evolved a bit and they talk about Cynthia having "that conversation" with the network. With her partner's advice and encouragement, Cathy has found a less aggressive way of being herself.

Eleanor has told her mother she quite likes Cynthia. Cathy can't decide whether that's true, but she appreciates it. Richard has persuaded Florence to say nothing. The June wedding is on track – and *everyone* has been invited.

There seem to be several university architecture departments in the Bay Area that are willing to take Florence. Andrew worries about their marrying so young, and at a stage of Richard's career where he will rarely be home for dinner. Eleanor pointed out that he and Cathy had done approximately the same thing. "Not much of a recommendation," he told his older daughter – but after that he shut up about it.

Joe and Sally live in London. She has "repackaged herself" – Joe's words – as a fashionable hostess. Andrew hasn't asked what that entails. Joe continues to find the British absurd. Figuring out how to integrate his own and Shiva's business interests requires Joe to work long hours and travel a lot. Sally disciplines him if he doesn't get home when he promised. Joe continues to find that inexplicably satisfying.

Shiva and the Governor have essentially become best friends. The local newspaper published a picture of the two of them at a black-tie charity function under the headline, "Boston Brahmins," which was inevitable. Rosemary had the clipping framed and hung it in her library. "My two boys," she explains when visitors notice it.

"They share the disability," she says, "or maybe it's a gift, of a massive sense of entitlement – which Shiva regards as his patrimony and George as a form of patriotism." She isn't bitter, just perceptive. "I'm no better," she adds. "I've gotten whatever men I wanted my whole life. I just haven't wanted the right one until now."

Rosemary continues to live in New York. Shiva let her have the apartment with the chef and the maid and the butler. She goes to Boston some weekends, and sometimes they meet in Nantucket. "I am not a nice person," she likes to say, "but I'm not stupid either." She realised that so long as the Governor never entirely possessed her, he would never lose interest – and she doesn't want him to do so. George has let it be known that she has declined his repeated proposals of marriage. Voters find that romantic.

It has not been necessary to tell them who Judy is. Judy says that simplifies things for now

Joe pointed out to Andrew that thinking up deals could be done anywhere. Andrew said he'd probably be more creative if he *wasn't* near Wall Street. He and Janis intend to settle in Boston. Judy and Janis continue to be best friends.

Janis never went back to the Governor's office, nor did she look for another job. She and Andrew stayed in Nantucket through the summer, honouring the invitations he had outstanding, and then into the fall because they could. They haven't "retired," but agreed they had "other priorities" – like getting acquainted. Judy explained the concept to Janis in an early postcard from India: "Marriage is school. You have to do the homework."

You would have to say they've been diligent. They found the right blend of tenderness and honesty from the start. When they got upstairs, they went instinctively to the bunkroom. Its narrow beds were the only ones with neither occupants nor associations. "Do you want…?" he said.

"Of course," she said.

"I mean, this isn't St. Elizabeth's, even if it looks like a dormitory. We're not required to do what Rosemary says. We're both on the rebound from…unusual relationships," he said. "I'm not sure we can trust our emotions."

"Then we'll have to trust our bodies," she said. "And no more talking."

The house had a lot of left-over angst in it, so he didn't take her downstairs the next morning to watch the dawn. "Plenty of time for that," he said.

"Kissing?" she said.

"Of course."

Janis tackled Cathy right after breakfast. Andrew wouldn't have been able to. She contrived to have the conversation in a place where Andrew could overhear them, though. "I assume you will want to stay in your apartment in New York," she said.

"I suppose we will," said Cathy.

"Do you mind if I stay here?"

"I don't see how I can object."

"Do you mind if Andrew and I make changes – that is, if he wants to? Personally, I think the way you've decorated the house is perfect, but there might be things Andrew wanted to do."

"To mark his territory?"

"To recover his balance."

"He has gone a bit wobbly, hasn't he?"

Janis didn't answer that.

"Florence won't like it if it isn't the house she remembers," said Cathy.

Janis took a deep breath. Andrew put down the newspaper he was pretending to read, ready to intervene. "If you don't mind my saying so," said Janis, "and to be honest, even if you do, this family has a talent for getting into stuck."

"We aren't going to be friends, are we?" said Cathy.

"No," said Janis.

"But you're right," said Cathy. "So, fine."

In the event, Andrew didn't need to make any changes. Knowing he could turned out to be sufficient.

The cleaners Joe hired arrived at midday. They came in an SUV full of vacuum cleaners and garbage bags. "He said he was going to do that," Andrew said with a laugh.

Somewhat unexpectedly, Cathy, Cynthia and Rosemary took the afternoon ferry back and hired a taxi to drive them to New York. "I think we're rich now," said Cynthia. "We can afford it." All three of them giggled.

Rosemary declined Cathy's offer of a guest room and checked into the Four Seasons for a week. "I need to go into my cave for a while," she explained. George called her the second night, and joined her on Friday. Nothing dramatic happened in Massachusetts that weekend, which disappointed the Lieutenant Governor.

Andrew drove George to the airport for the afternoon flight

to Boston. The Governor said he couldn't hang about waiting for Lydia's movers to finish. And though he didn't mention it, he didn't have any staff anymore. What if he has to issue a statement? Andrew said to himself. George at least had known better than to ask Janis if she was coming.

"I didn't steal Rosemary," said the Governor after they got in the car. "I hope you recognise that."

"I do," said Andrew.

"Good."

That seemed to be the end of it, but a few minutes down the road he spoke again: "You think you'll get along with Janis?"

"Yes."

"That's good too," said the Governor.

The thought came to Andrew that the next time he saw George they would both pretend the weekend had never happened, and their friendship would continue as before – provided of course that it didn't trouble Janis. "It's like being friends with a lion," he told her later. "It's an honour. But you do what the lion wants."

"Believe me," she said, "I understand that."

"So, can he be our friend?" said Andrew, surprised to discover that he cared.

"Give it a couple of months," she said. He didn't like that answer, and she could see that he didn't. "It's nothing to do with us," she said. "I just need the bruises to heal."

"You think there's going to be an 'us?'"

"I do," she said.

Andrew had stopped at the store on the way back and bought a cooked chicken, a box of dinner rolls and fresh salad makings. Janis had said they needed "new food." Alone in the house for nearly an hour, she'd thrown out everything in the refrigerator. Then she just sat in the living room and waited for Andrew to come back.

"I *insist* on there being an 'us,'" she continued. "I didn't like your not being here. And by the way, there was a lot of creaking."

"Wood contracts when the temperature goes down," said Andrew.

"Ghosts came out of the walls," said Janis.

"Monsters?"

"A few," she said. "But there are always monsters to contend with. We can deal with them. And there have been happy times here too. Those ghosts look forward to Florence's wedding. We'll have to get them new sheets."

"Richard and Florence?"

"No, silly, the happy ghosts."

Andrew laughed at that. They were sitting on the sofa where two days earlier he'd watched Shiva interview Janis about Judy while Cynthia hid upstairs contemplating mayhem and everyone else made dinner. That seemed like the distant past. Andrew had his arms around Janis now. He'd wanted to do that then but hadn't let himself acknowledge it. "This feels right," he said. "You feel right."

"My body is exactly where it wants to be," she said.

"How did this happen?" said Andrew.

"It's a magical island, remember?"

"I must write a thank-you note to Shiva for releasing the magic," said Andrew. "Have you spoken to Judy? I mean, it's all right if you do."

"I have."

"And?"

"She'll be in London by now."

"I mean about us."

"She says it was obvious."

"What did you say?"

"I said it sort of crept up on me. Crept in a good way, you understand. You were so easy to talk to. I liked the sound of your voice."

"I felt the same way," said Andrew.

"Let's have dinner," she said. "I'm starving."

They went into the kitchen. "I'll be in charge of the chicken," he said, "if you'll be in charge of the salad."

"And afterwards," she said, "we'll put our bodies in charge."

"Wine?" said Andrew. "Just a glass to relax us."

"No," said Janis. "I want to feel everything."

"Brave," said Andrew.

"Brave together," said Janis.

They set about making dinner. Andrew's brain was suddenly awash in imagined music, full of minor chords and hesitations, which seemed to be approaching a conclusion. He thought about the choices and accidents that had brought them together in a house that had known so much hope and sadness over the years.

"What would you have done if Rosemary hadn't decided to change partners last night?" he asked. Probably not a smart question to ask, he realised.

Janis had her back to him and she didn't answer right away. She turned around slowly. "Murdered her," she said.

Andrew attempted not to cry. "It's just, I've been quite lonely."

"Me too," said Janis, putting her arms around him.

The invisible musicians put down their instruments.

Also by Harrison Young

Also by Harrison Young